Journal entry #41

He's met some new ladies. They *bought* him. Paid for his time and attention. Things he could be bestowing on me. That is, if he knew how much I wanted his notice, needed him in my life.

But no. He has no clue.

There have been a few times I've tried to get through to him, but to no avail.

It sucks.

This time though I think I've found a different way to get to him.

Time to put my plans in motion.

The following story is a work of fiction. All names, characters, and places are products of the author's imagination or are used in a fictitious manner. Any resemblance, including but not limited, to actual events, locales, organizations, or persons, living or dead, is entirely coincidental.

Tracked
Copyright © 2012 Casey Moss
ISBN-10: 0985459905
ISBN-13: 978-0-9854599-0-1
E-Book Numbers Venue Assigned
THP Publishing & THP Designs

DEDICATION

A big thank you to Terri Valentine for mentoring me when I took my first steps in the world of publishing and showing me the way. I'd also like to acknowledge my author pals—Erin Sinclair, Johanna Riley, RM Sotera & Shannan Albright—who helped me out with updating this project from its previous version, *Concealed Affairs*, in addition to being there on personal levels as well. Your friendships are appreciated more than you know! And, as always, my heart and gratitude to CJM, whose love and support of my goals keeps me going.

~ Casey

TRACKED

CASEY MOSS

"YOU CAN'T RUN AND YOU CAN'T HIDE. I CAN TRACK YOU WITH EASE."

PROLOGUE

Journal entry #38

Some call me weird. I've heard the whispers that I'm crazy. I'm not.

I want him near me like I have never wanted anything in my life. Dreams of having his arms around me plague my every thought. I can't control my driving urge to be with him. Emotion takes over and I see nothing, know nothing but my compulsion to get back to him. I would do anything to be with him. Be the center of his world. I would do *anything* to…Get. Him. Back.

That is my wish, my want, my absolute need. With thoughts focusing on when we'll be together, all else fades from my mind. My fantasies run rampant. I imagine him stepping forward and claiming me. Telling me everything I want to hear. Oh, my imagination is fantastic, but I can't wait until it's for real.

To see him but not be able to be near him, touch him, is the madness. Oh, I've tried to get to him, but haven't had any luck. God, I hurt inside when I can't see him, and it seems like forever between the times I do. Doesn't he understand what's going on with me? I pray one day he'll *wake up* and see the truth. And when he does, we will become inseparable. I will please him. With him I will love and be loved. Finally.

That there are friends who would help me obtain my heart's desire pleases me. My heart sings with joy that there are kind people in the world still. Luckily, I've been fortunate to find them. He and I are destined to be with each other. Otherwise, why would God have sent me assistance?

What displeases me, though, is there are people who would conspire against me, hinder my plans to be with him. Why should anyone but him have a say in who he loves and does not love? Why should they keep him from me? He should be the only one to make the choice who he wants to be with (me) and who he loves (me, of course). No one else should do it for him or interfere in our relationship. The fact they do hinder my plans to be with him makes me angry.

The hot as hell, see red, there better be no sharp objects around, kind of mad.

Gah! People!

Just thinking of everyone and their troublesome ways has my blood pressure spiking, the rage roiling within me. The so-called experts say that journaling one's thought process and feelings is supposed to be therapeutic. It's bullshit. I'm more riled now than when I started this stupid entry.

Anyone who interferes will pay. They'll pay dearly.

CHAPTER ONE

I can't believe I'm here.

Gritting her teeth, Victoria Padden gripped the brass railing of the second floor balcony while her boss and friend, Sally, waited in line to enter the hotel's conference room. The crowd in the building's grand foyer below bustled with activity. Employees and hotel patrons battled through the nattering sea of bodies. Women's voices echoed in the huge contemporary-styled lobby with a greenhouse roof ceiling and rang in her head. The din wasn't enough to cover her irritated thoughts though.

She should have turned tail and ran the moment the poster boards in the hotel entrance advertising the bachelor auction came into view. Sally, apparently sensing her intent to escape, had clutched her arm, inhibiting her chance to flee.

Rubbing the tender area on her bicep, she cast a glance over her shoulder. The older woman's thin lips pressed into a smug grin, enhancing the small laugh lines around her eyes.

Of course she'd be pleased with herself. She tricked me into coming. Networking with other business people while at a fundraiser. Sure. What good could come out of something like this when you're not into it? With a huff, she turned and rested her back against the banister.

"Yes?" Sally flashed a smile and winked. Her tailored midnight blue dress suit, though contrasting against the non-descript beige wall outside the conference room and multi-colored patterned carpet, enhanced her eyes and blonde hair.

Her boss' amusement didn't help her mood. "I can't believe you *ordered* me to come to this." Displeased, Victoria swept her arm out over the railing, indicating the swarm of giddy women down below and gathering in the wide hall, waiting to enter the event. "I thought you were my friend. I thought you knew me better."

Sally didn't seem to take notice of the bite in her words. She continued to smile as if being away from the office wasn't a big deal. "I *am* your friend, Tori, but as your *boss*, you left me no choice. All you want to do is work. Not that I mind, but all work and no play…" She waved a well-manicured hand in the air. "Anyway, we're here, and I'm glad we arrived early. There's a horde of people below. Must be over a hundred women in attendance this year. Could you imagine if we had come in now? Lucky for us, there's barely anyone ahead in line, so we should be able to find some good seats."

"Still, you know how I hate these things. Rich women with no thought of anybody but themselves. Acting haughty, viewing other people as *below their status*. The gossip. It all makes my teeth itch."

Sally rolled her eyes and plucked a piece of lint off the silk sleeve of her designer jacket. "Events like this irritate you because you can't let go of your past. I understand the hurt you felt when your parents planned a social climbing party for your college graduation, which overshadowed your success from the accomplishment. I know how your peers in New York viewed you as subpar. So what if you didn't want to follow in their footsteps? You carved out a career in the IT field instead of marrying rich and wasting days away at luncheons and in spas. Fortunate for me, of course. But try to get over all that and remember how to enjoy life, okay?"

Her boss turned around and moved forward with the line toward a couple of tables.

Curious, Victoria counted the women in front of them. Fifty heads. She looked at Sally again, who spoke with an attendee. Her boss smiled so brightly, Victoria thought of her as a child who had a secret to share.

Sally was right. She had to find her balance again. That nice sweet spot between being too serious and too fun-loving party girl. Her animosity dissipated. She was at a bachelor auction. Big deal. No one here knew her or her parents. She wouldn't have to live up to anyone's grand expectations. Perhaps she could even sit back and *enjoy* a socialite event for once. If all went well, she would call her mother. She'd be pleased to hear about her daughter's escapade with Princeton society, no matter what the jaunt entailed.

She smiled as pleasing thoughts buzzed in her head and imagined her parents' faces full of pride. Yet, as quickly as their images appeared, a scowling one replaced them.

David. Crap. Telling that prudish man she went to a bachelor auction would be another matter entirely. Not that it should be an issue. They barely were boyfriend/girlfriend anymore.

She closed her eyes and prayed none of his patients or clinic associates were in attendance, and if any were, they wouldn't recognize her from the picture he kept on his desk…if it still was on his desk that is… If word got back to him, she didn't know how she'd explain this little excursion of Sally's.

"If David knew what I was up to, he'd have a fit," she muttered, displeased she wasn't at the place she enjoyed most, in her chair at her desk staring at the computer screen. Coming here was not a good idea.

"You act as if you're married," Sally retorted. "Give me your hands."

Not wanting Sally to cause a scene, Tori stepped forward and offered her hands, palms up.

Sally took them, turned them over and studied the back of them. "Just as I thought. No rings. I see there's no leash tied around your neck either. Guess you're still broken up."

Victoria straightened her spine and glared at her friend. "Trial separation. We still have feelings for each other." *Well, at least I* think *we do.*

"Relax, Tori." Sally's teal-eyed gaze narrowed. "You're on a break. David doesn't have to know. You don't have to tell him. You're here to have fun, to break the monotony of your everyday routine. Add some spice to your life."

Geez, what's going on here? Not tell David? Yeah, right. Tori's thoughts swirled. Though fifteen years of age separated them, she and Sally were great friends, sharing their sorrows and joys, being there for each other, valuing the other's opinion. Usually her boss understood her pretty well. Sally knew she'd have to tell David. Relationships were based on trust, not secrets. Yet, kind, caring Sally, who had taken her under her wing when she had been fresh out of college, acted no where near kind or caring, or even very understanding, at the moment.

"You're a puppet, Tori," Sally continued. "A maid. I'd even say a slave who is constantly under David's control. You should have stayed put in your own house, never moved in with that man. Good thing you moved out."

"Excuse me? I don't see myself as any of those things. David's basically good. I'm happy with him and doing things for him. We're comfortable together."

"Liar." With a huff, Sally turned away.

"He has an ABD in Psychiatry and has patients lining up to see him at the clinic," Victoria ranted to Sally's back. "I have my career. We're both financially stable. We're both emotionally stable as well. We've just hit a blip and decided not to live together anymore. At the end of the day, I go to his house, straighten the place up and make him dinner. After he comes home, he tells me about his day. There's nothing to complain about, and we never really fight."

"Uh-huh. So you keep saying and reminding me. Life with him sounds positively wonderful and exciting." Sally's voice dripped with sarcasm. She moved forward with the line and didn't turn around. "That's why you've cooled things and moved back to your place."

Tori decided to keep her mouth shut. She and David for the most part had enjoyed a set routine. No surprises, no changes. Except a month ago she had brought up the *M* word. David said they'd talk about marriage at some point, but every time she tried, he'd hedge. The lack of communication, their jobs, his schooling…their almost non-existent sex life…all the stresses ate at their relationship. They decided to take a step back instead of forward.

Too bad she had mentioned the *M*-word conversation to her friend. What a big mistake that had been. Not liking David to begin with, Sally hadn't been pleased the word marriage had come up. That day their differences had been aired and a small rift had formed in their friendship. For the past month, Sally had made one criticism after another about her and David's relationship.

And she'd borne them all.

Being with someone was better than being alone. Wasn't it?

"Earth to Tori. Stop your daydreaming. We're almost to the table and when we get there we'll be able to check out the *merchandise*." She waggled her brows.

"That's crude, Sally."

"When did you turn into such a priss? Oh, wait. David. Taking lessons from him again, are we?" Sally asked, snickering. "You used to be so much fun, but don't worry. I'm the one who's bidding here, not you."

"What does your husband have to say about this?"

"Nothing."

Tori quirked an eyebrow and cocked her head in silent question.

Sally sighed. "I planned to tell Frank. Then I figured, why bother? I've been at him for the past year to take care of stuff around the house. I'm tired of talking to a brick wall. So I decided to take matters into my own hands and hire someone again." Arriving at the tables covered in silver-colored cloth, Sally emitted a school-girl giggle. "Here we are. Tori, come, look and see who we'll be bidding on. The charity coordinators have put together a really nice auction this year." Sally traced her finger over a paper attached to a clipboard, then sorted through some photographs in an album. "Hmm, I even happen to know a few of the men."

Tori snorted, not seeing the point in checking out the *merchandise* when she didn't plan to participate, and stepped back from the table, jostling against some women standing around. She took a deep breath to calm her exasperation. *God, why can't I get into a better mood?*

At the table, a middle aged woman with taut features and no wrinkles, most likely from one too many face-lifts and injections, asked Sally for their names.

"Victoria Padden and Sally Becker. I'm Sally. Sourpuss here is Victoria," Sally said, jerking her thumb in her direction.

Tori turned her head to the side, refusing to acknowledge Sally's dig at her expense, nor the fact that she couldn't shake a feeling of doom. Her need-to-please, usually happy-go-lucky personality had taken one too many hits already. She'd like Sally to be proud of the work she could do. She needed her friend to like her significant other, no matter who he was. She wished she could be happy about being out of the office which would make Sally happy, but nothing was turning out like it should.

"Have you been to one of our bachelor auctions before, Ms. Becker?"

"Oh, yes, plenty of times."

"Glad to have you back then. Here are your packets and markers. You're number one-ten and Ms. Padden is one-eleven. Have a good time."

"Thanks." Taking Tori's arm, Sally added, "Come along." With a pull, she dragged her into the conference hall.

The room was much larger and brighter than Tori expected. Hundreds of black folding chairs sat in precise lines in front of an immense stage in the overly illuminated area. Flowing, gauze-like white and silver material hid the walls of the conference room. Crimson curtains hung from the ceiling to the stage floor on each side of the platform, separating the attendees from the backstage activities. Without resistance on Tori's part, Sally led her down a red carpet runner aisle to a couple of seats five rows back from the grand platform and handed her the bag of information.

"One year, the men walked down the aisle and were close enough to pinch. Then they went up the stairs right there in front and did their cat walk," Sally said, showing the path they took with two wiggling fingers. "So it went till all twenty-five bachelors were auctioned off. Too bad the method had to be changed. One gentleman's rear was so bruised from the pinching he couldn't sit the rest of the day. At least that's what I had heard."

Tori tossed the auction material onto the floor under her chair. She shifted in her seat. David wouldn't like this at all. He'd tell her ogling men was repulsive, that bidding on a person, especially a man, and pinching his backside to boot was degrading. She shook her head to clear David's voice from her thoughts. He wasn't here. He didn't have to know she'd been here. Hell, he wasn't talking to her anyway, so what did all the internal chatter matter?

"Last year, this auction raised almost thirty-five thousand dollars for the Women's Counseling Center and shelters," a woman next to her offered. "This year they hope to raise just as much."

"That's nice," Tori replied, hoping to hear a bit more, but the woman had already turned her focus to another person.

At least the money goes for a good cause. She stood to smooth down the wrinkles in her skirt and sat again.

"The auction should be starting. Why can't all those women hurry up and get in here? Folding chairs are not the most comfortable seats," she mumbled, peeking at her watch.

As she stood to readjust again, her attention honed in on movement at the side of the stage. Fingers gripped the edges of the heavy curtain, held them apart a couple of inches. She gasped and dropped down into the hard chair, having sworn she saw a pair of eyes watching her from behind the curtain.

Not just watching…studying…like they'd been casing the place…me. She glanced around. *I was the only one standing in my area, that's why they honed in on me. That's it. That's all that was. That's all it can be.*

The curtain swished back into place.

After all, Steve's still away…

"Excuse me."

A gruff voice from the aisle startled her out of her thoughts. "Sally, get a load of this," she whispered, her gaze widening in surprise as a man, with a marker in his hand, worked his way down the row of already filled chairs in front of her and Sally. He sat down. "That man is going to bid. Do you think he's…" She tilted her flattened hand side to side.

"Oh, dear." Sally chuckled. "Didn't I explain the auction to you?"

"No. You pulled me aside at work, told me we'd be going out for the afternoon. You made me believe this fundraiser excursion was for business. The only conversation we had about coming revolved my excuses being knocked down by you, and you making my attendance to this event mandatory. How did you put it? *Business is business, whether you're here or there.*"

"Nice impersonation. Remind me not to let you answer my phone in the office or else people might mistake you for me."

Tori shared in Sally's laughter, then continued, "Anyway, as for this auction, I'm gathering a woman bids on a man and the one who bids highest in effect hires him. Then he performs *services* for her."

Sally gasped and shook her head. "Tori, Tori, Tori... Not *those* kinds of services. This is all legit. Each man has a specific service and depending upon what you need done determines which man you bid on. Take for example, Mrs. Drake, who's here somewhere." Sally surveyed the area. "She wants her portrait done whether it's sketched, photographed, or painted, it doesn't matter. She'll focus on the men with tulip corsages. Now, in my case, I need a man who's good with his hands. You know carpenter, handy-man, a jack-of-all-trades type, so I'll focus on those with the red roses."

"God, I feel stupid." She bowed her head and eyed the deep purple and gold patterns of the carpet at her feet.

"Don't worry about it, honey. My first time, I thought the same thing. Actually, I hoped it was like that."

"Sally!" She jerked up her head and gaped at her friend. Frank and Sally were a power couple. She looked up to them and hoped to emulate their relationship with a man in her life. To think Sally would stray from such a great relationship… She couldn't.

"Don't Sally me. It was over ten years ago. Frank and I were having trouble, and I thought a little fun was what I needed. What I ended up with, though, was a beautiful flower garden. I've been coming to this event ever since."

"And you've only *now* invited me?"

"Didn't have a reason to up till now."

"What?" The overhead lights darkened and her question disappeared into the thundering applause. She made a mental note to ask Sally later what she had meant by her remark.

Loud techno music blared from the four corners of the hall. Drawn into the upbeat music, Victoria clapped and cheered along with everyone else around her.

ॐॐॐॐॐॐ

A spotlight swept the stage, then landed on a podium in the corner. The clapping and cheering of the gathering crescendoed to a frenzied pace until a pretty gray-haired woman walked into the light and held up her arms, gesturing for order. The crowd fell into silence.

"Welcome, ladies and gentlemen," the woman's mature, nasally voice boomed over the loud speakers. "Thank you all for coming and supporting our great cause. As a reminder, the minimum bid is five hundred dollars and the more you donate, the longer the hired service lasts. With the money you donate today, battered women and their children, who are in need of help, will continue to have a safe haven to go to with trained counselors on site. Bid generously and let the auction begin!"

More high-pitched, excited cheers rang through the hall. As the music died away and the lights brightened, a thin, elderly gentleman dressed in jeans, a blue denim dress shirt and straw cowboy hat sauntered out and took the woman's spot. He picked up a gavel, rapped the device on the podium and called out the first bachelor's name.

Victoria smiled and perched on the edge of her chair, surprised at the wave of anticipation flooding through her. Sally was right. She had become overly reserved. She used to be such a wild woman, always in search of the next party, the next guy, the next fun activity. A long time had passed since she let go and had let herself enjoy life. Wanting to thank Sally, she turned, only to find her friend's gaze narrowed and a look of disgust on her face.

"Sally? What is it?"

"It's Gertrude Sims," Sally whispered, leaning toward Tori. "She comes every year hoping to catch a husband for her daughter, Bertha. Wicked woman, and her daughter's just as bad. They think because they have money they can buy anything they want or treat anyone anyway they want. I have a feeling I know who she'll be after this year."

"Who?" The prospect of seeing Sally in a bidding war engulfed her with more excitement.

"His name is Geoff McKenzie, a very handsome and intelligent businessman. He and his cousin, Philip, are partners in a prominent general contracting and landscaping business. I hear he's very skilled with his hands, so he'll be wearing a rose." Puffing up like a peacock, she added, "I'll save the gentleman from those two harridans."

"Where are they?"

"Across the way." Sally pointed with her chin to a place behind Tori. "On the outside aisle, two rows back."

Tori looked over her right shoulder and shivered. The obese older woman dressed in a flimsy and frilly, almost transparent, light lilac-colored dress had topped off her outfit with a huge, garish matching hat complete with a lilac feather on the side. Mortified on the woman's behalf, her hand flew to her mouth to cover her shock. *Who told her that outfit looked good on her?* Even more disturbing—the young woman with her. The daughter dressed identical to the mother but in light blue.

Too bad Sally couldn't save all the men from those two.

Victoria willed her attention back to the proceedings and rubbed her eyebrows hoping to dispel the pastel imagery that seemed to have burned itself on her retinas. When the horrid vision had finally gone, she realized the hall seemed unnaturally quiet. A good portion of the audience was subdued as one man after another walked the stage with uninteresting airs. Only a few bids rang out on the men wearing white carnations. Sally, too, sat silently, tapping her marker against her leg.

Tori bent over and retrieved Sally's pamphlet from beneath her friend's chair. She scanned the pages for the descriptions of the flowers the men had pinned to them. The current one on stage, who wore the white flower as well, was involved in accounting services. Since tax season wasn't for several

⪧⪦⪧⪦⪧⪦⪧

months, she didn't believe the men wearing those flowers would bring in much to the charity. She put the pamphlet back under the chair.

She had to admit, the first six men to appear were quite handsome, even if they were a bit dull. Where were they when she was out in the dating pool? She shook her head. No matter. Life couldn't be better. She was...

Her heart caught in her throat. The seventh man strutted across the stage with a righteous air of command. With long powerful strides, he crossed back again and stood right before her.

She held her breath and clutched at the drumming in her neck. In all her life, she had never seen such a fine-looking man. Thick waves of sable hair were combed back into place behind his ears and the longer locks cascaded down to touch the rim of his collar. Slightly curved brows enhanced dark eyes which sat above chiseled cheeks in perfect symmetry and a strong, squared chin. The tailored-cut, deep myrtle-colored suit, complimented his bronzed skin and defined his broad shoulders and narrow waist.

Man, I bet he's beautiful nude. With a start, she mentally shook off the gush of feminine awareness running rampant in her body. Her focus settled on the red rose he wore on his right lapel. *Forget that McKenzie guy. Surely God meant for me to bid on him. Otherwise, He wouldn't have seen fit to put the man of my dreams before me.* While watching him hold up his large masculine hands, she cautiously tried to grab the marker from Sally.

Her friend's hand and marker weren't there.

Tori's hand snapped back as if she had touched a hot stove. She looked down at her empty extremity in astonishment, then back at the man on stage. His eyes, sparkling from the stage lights, met hers. Lost in their warm depths, the auctioneer's voice faded away, and the loud drumming of her heart drowned out the women's bids.

The in and out movements of his arms as he appeared to ask the women to pick him beckoned to her. In her mind, he begged her to join him, and so help her, she wanted to. She wanted those large strong hands on her, to touch her in places lovers touch. She wanted to know the man behind those wonderful eyes, wanted to know him thoroughly. A heated wave of desire coursed through her. Moisture settled at the juncture of her thighs. She shifted in her seat. For the first time in her life, she understood what the phrase to fall in love at first sight meant.

As if hearing her thoughts, an expression of knowing flashed in his eyes and his face creased into a devilish smile. He winked at her, then sauntered off the stage. She stared at his retreating form in shock.

Love? Not possible. The idea went against all logic to be able to fall love with someone so quickly. But if the feeling wasn't love, then what? What else could make a person's body ignite like it was on fire, cause a heart to speed recklessly, to become breathless?

Lust.

"Oh, my God," she mouthed in a hushed whisper realizing that because of her time with David that she'd almost forgotten what desire felt like.

She slumped her shoulders and through lowered lids glanced about. No one gawked at her so no one had noticed her reactions to the man on stage. She heaved a sigh of relief. At least she had caught her thoughts in time and recognized her body's responses for what they were.

Covering her eyes with her hands, she silently chided herself. How could she have let herself succumb and lose control to such primitive animalistic urges? Her actions weren't right, went against everything she believed in. *Against the very core of one's moral worth*, as David would say. She should have kept better control of herself, not have gotten caught up in all the excitement. Now what would she do and say if

෯෯෯෯෯෯

David found out where she had been? If she lied, he'd see right through her. He'd know somehow.

Stuck in the circle of her thoughts, she barely noticed Sally's long fingers gripping her arm again.

"Come along, Victoria. We have to pay for our prize."

She stood, hoping her trembling legs wouldn't buckle beneath her. Only twice before had a man unnerved her as much as that man had, and that had been years ago when she shared her first kiss with her first boyfriend. The second time…well, that had been so traumatic she still didn't like to think about it. And seeing those eyes peer out between the curtain folds had almost brought those memories back.

"But… I thought… Don't you have to bid on that McKenzie fellow?" she asked, flustered over her silliness. Sally led her away from the audience to a door adjoining the ballroom.

"That *was* the McKenzie fellow," her boss replied with a chuckle, opening the way.

CHAPTER TWO

*I*gnoring everyone and everything around him, Geoff hurried to a secluded corner. "What the hell am I doing here?" he sputtered and collapsed into a chair. He placed his elbows on his knees, curled all ten of his fingers in his hair and pulled.

"Don't be nervous, Geoff," said a perky young volunteer passing by. "It's a charity event for a very worthy cause. You should be honored."

Honored. Sure. Having been told the one to bid highest on him would receive free repair work around her place and the money would go to a woman's charity, he had agreed to participate believing his participation would be good for business. Only later did he learn from another bachelor—right before the event started—that the event was more of a high priced dating service for wealthy, older women, or mothers looking for husbands for their daughters than a charity event.

It was the newspaper scenario from two years ago, all over again. He should never have had agreed to that, either. Yet, when a reporter from the local paper had called him, pitching a story about the area's most eligible bachelors, his only thought then, too, had been how the article would be good for business. He had never imagined the bundles of mail and the many phone calls the feature would generate. And, fool he was, he had chosen to respond to a few.

The first letter he had acted on had been Cindy's. She had been a pleasant and intelligent companion. With an eye for interior design, she had helped him redecorate his office. A few months into their relationship, though, she had stopped returning his calls.

Then there was Andrea. Adventurous and beautiful enough to be a supermodel, he had been the envy of other men with her on his arm. Even his cousin, Philip, had been jealous. The relationship with her had lasted only a few months before she, too, had disappeared without a word.

The last one he had contacted was Nina, a third year college student in a five-year program for engineering. She had been a bit young for him, but she'd had a good head on her shoulders and was mature beyond her years. That affair, lasting the longest at seven months, had ended after he'd called her dorm room one night and her roommate had informed him that she'd had gotten scared and went back home. He asked what had frightened her, but Nina's roommate wanted no involvement in the situation and had hung up.

The situation. He had no clue what she had meant by that, no idea what spooked the women. It was all too strange, and he never was able to get any answers.

He stopped dating after that. He had too much going on in his life to try to figure the women out or bother with romantic involvements. They weren't worth it. He should have learned his lesson years ago after his wife, Sue Ellen, had taken off. Women always left him high and dry, and always the perfect gentleman, he didn't believe their *getting spooked* had anything to do with him first hand.

The noise in the room grew louder, but not loud enough to drown out his troubling thoughts. He gripped his hair tighter. If he hadn't been so damn curious to see how large the crowd was and so nervous with stage fright, he wouldn't have checked out the audience before the event had started. He wouldn't have felt like he was sucker punched in the gut.

Geoff's heart thundered in his ears as it had before and during his time on the stage. He should have known they would be here—the old, heavyset woman in her gaudy clothes along with her equally pudgy daughter. He should have requested a list of patrons. That way he could have known who would be out there, and he never would have set foot out in the limelight. Hindsight was twenty-twenty and a bitch. And, this time, he didn't have a choice in the pickings, the women did. His skin crawled with the thought.

Those two women had been thorns in his side from the moment the article had been published. Mrs. Sims, who constantly harangued him regarding her daughter, Bertha, kept persisting with phone calls, letters, pictures and comments through mutual business associates. She had the idea in her mind that he and Bertha would make quite a pair and couldn't understand why he didn't want her.

Every time he had started seeing someone new, he made sure the two women learned about his new relationship because, stupidly, he assumed once they knew he was involved, they would stop bothering him. But, no, he hadn't been destined to be that lucky. They had continued their pursuits, the two vultures circling their prey, waiting for him to give up and give in to their whims.

During his search of the audience, his attention had passed them over, and he had focused on a very lovely young woman. He had believed she would be his saving grace. Out on stage, he had made sure to get her attention focused on him. He had given her one of his most irresistible smiles and never let his gaze leave hers.

His tactics hadn't worked.

How could she not have bid on him? He had portrayed his best features—his strut, his body, his hands, even his secret weapon smile. Had she raised her number? No, not once. She had just sat there staring at him like a doe caught in a car's headlights.

Releasing his grip on his hair, he rubbed his palms against his pants, then his temples. He hated to do it, but he had to resign himself to his sentence of hell with the crazed duo or some other matron. There was no way out now.

৯০৪৯০৪৯০৪

"This is what a guy gets when he tries to make a buck," he muttered with a shake of his head, chastising himself for being so gullible.

A few minutes later, the cheerful young volunteer came by again.

"Time to meet your new employer," she sang.

He slowly raised his head to see the thin blonde smiling down at him. How could she be so cheerful? Didn't she know the Simses? Didn't she realize they were vipers, the bane of everyone's existence? If she had any clue, that happy expression would instead be a look of pity, and she'd be offering condolences.

Oh, well. Time to face the music.

Dragging his body out of the chair and shuffling like a man in chains, he followed her to hear his sentence. All around him people talked and laughed while consuming aromatic, flavored coffee and pastries. The first several men, standing around with their new employers, appeared to be pleased with the matches. How could he enjoy the festivities, though, when he was being sent to hell, a man condemned to the sickening whims of Mrs. Sims and her equally offensive daughter? Or maybe some other mother/daughter pair who might be worse? The other bachelors' happiness cut at his soul, and the thick sweet smell of the baked goods turned his stomach.

His gaze diverted back to the table of destination. A breath of relief broke from his lips. The Simses were nowhere in sight. Instead, there stood a classy blonde and the one whom he had hoped would be his saving grace. Unburdened from an unseen weight, his shoulders lifted, and his frazzled nerves sprang back to proper form. He willed away the urge to fall to his knees and offer up prayers of thanks. He'd be damned if he ruined his one good suit.

"Three thousand for Mr. McKenzie."

He and his escort stopped in their tracks. He quickly calculated the numbers. For five hundred dollars to a grand, one weekend of time needed to be donated. A thousand to fifteen hundred, meant he'd incur two weekends, and for fifteen hundred it would be three. No one, from what he knew, had ever gone for more. Most bids stayed under eight hundred.

Maybe he *was* being sentenced to hell.

The woman must have some major project planned. He sized up the blonde who had said the amount. A large job could take time away from his duties. He mentally shrugged. If her task did pull him away from his projects, so be it. Doing excellent work, especially for a good cause, would lead to more referrals which, of course, would lead to more business. His mouth curved into a smile. More business meant more money which meant he'd continue to have a business of his own and keep his accounts in the black.

Perhaps this auction wasn't so bad an ordeal after all.

"That's the largest bid we've ever received," said the young blonde in awe.

Geoff returned the girl's smile, pleased he was able to bring such a sum. Seeing his *savior's* mouth hanging open amused him even more. He chuckled as the classy blonde put her hand up to her companion's chin and pushed her mouth closed.

The women turned their heads at the sound of his laughter. The elder's sharp eyes and determined facial expression had him catching his breath in his throat. His stomach clenched into a tight ball again. After a brief moment in which she seemed to assess him fully, she went back to her checkbook and paperwork.

His comfort zone shrank. Her money, her clothes, her demeanor spoke volumes. She was well off and probably a perfectionist. He didn't know what was worse, putting up with a matchmaker or someone like her. He figured she'd expect flawless, detailed service, not that it'd be a problem for him. If he were a betting man, he'd bet his business she wanted more from him than just a room painted.

With a flourish of her pen, the woman signed the check and handed the slip of paper to a speechless volunteer sitting at the table. Then with a flip of her hand, she motioned for him to join them.

Smoothing down his tousled hair, he straightened to his full six-feet-three-inches determined to show he couldn't be intimidated by her. He walked behind the woman and her pretty companion away from the table to an open area in the middle of the room.

"May I introduce myself and my friend?" The older woman held out her thin, three-ringed hand. "My name is Mrs. Sally Becker."

"Mrs. Becker." Geoff accepted her handshake.

"You can call me Sally. This is Victoria Padden."

His gaze was instantly drawn to Victoria's captivating blue eyes. He watched in wonder as her face colored to a hue a few shades lighter than the burgundy color dress suit she wore.

She was lovelier than he had first thought. Everything about her seemed to be graceful—the gentle arching of her eyebrows, the soft sculpture of her cheekbones and narrow short nose, and the smooth curving contours from her jaw line to her shoulders. His fingertips prickled. He wanted to see if the softness of her shoulder-length, wavy brown hair with blonde highlights felt as silky as the locks appeared.

He fought back the urge to caress her tresses and extended his hand in greeting. She hesitated, and when she did take his hand, he was surprised to receive a firm handshake in return. A pleasant tingling sensation nipped his fingers and palm, then crested up his arm. He kept their hands clasped together. He inclined his head and continued gazing into her eyes.

"Hello, Ms. Padden." He couldn't control his smile or his racing heart.

Her hello was barely audible.

He released her hand with reluctance.

"Please," her voice came soft and shy, "call me Victoria. Or Tori if you'd like."

"Tori, you can call me Geoff."

His heart hammered foolishly like he was a teenager out on a hot date. And as much as he wanted to bask in the reawakened sense of youth the woman made him feel, his mind told him to beware, not to succumb to thoughts and feelings which could only lead to hurt. With a deep breath to shuck off his thoughts, he turned to Sally.

"Mr. McKenzie, you're most likely wondering what you've gotten yourself into after hearing my winning bid amount. Well, if I were you, I wouldn't worry yourself over it. You'll not be indentured to me for life, nor for anything too major. Let's just say my bidding was a bit of a personal battle against another patron, and if my thinking is correct, you're happy I've won."

"Yes. Quite." He chuckled, relieved she was more pleasant than he'd originally believed. "You've taken a load off my mind, Sally. You have no idea." Geoff shook her hand in appreciation. Once he released Sally's hand, he couldn't resist a peek at her blushing friend.

He yearned to touch Tori again. To see if the sensation he had experienced wasn't a one-time thing, he placed his hand on her arm. A spark, albeit faint, pinched his palm.

"It was a pleasure meeting you, Tori."

She froze like a statue, her wide-eyed gaze on his face. She didn't reply.

This is interesting. Talk about being struck dumb. He knew his looks and mannerisms affected women, but she seemed fazed beyond normal limits. Then again, she stirred his feelings more than he wanted to admit.

Sally told him she'd call, then tugged on the *statue's* sleeve. Eventually she broke through Tori's stony countenance to take her away. In a matter of seconds, his pretty vision was gone.

Geoff slapped his palm against his forehead. *What the hell am I doing here?*

* * * *

Outside the room, Tori's legs, the consistency of jelly, quivered. Geoff McKenzie was the third man in her life to have such an affect on her. Even when she had met David for the first time he hadn't stunned her the way that man had. With David, their meeting had been a pleasant sense of comfort and her body had kept on an even till. There hadn't been an electrifying sense of attraction muddling her brain and sparking her nerves. Beginning with a touch, Geoff had finished the total destruction of her insides when his deep timbre voice spoke her name and vibrated within her core.

She shook her head to clear her mind.

"Quite a man, isn't he?" Traces of laughter tinged Sally's words.

Victoria bobbed her head. The tingling sensation she had experienced during the handshake returned, running through her fingers and arm. Goosebumps broke out in the tingle's wake.

Why did he have to be so charming? How had she managed not to make a total fool of herself? The situation was bad enough when she had forgotten what to do when he extended his hand, acting as if all her business training had never happened. But to lose her voice and her motor skills? She had never, ever lost her resolve so completely because a man had smiled in her direction.

"Yeah, a fine man." *A fine man, indeed.*

He seemed to know exactly what buttons to push to alter her mind and body, reducing all logic and sensible thought to a muddy mix. Those abilities weren't right. No man should have such powers over a woman.

David surely didn't.

ॐ∽ॐ∽ॐ∽ॐ

David. Damn. For a little while she had forgotten all about him. By now, he would be home wondering where she was. She had to compose herself. David would know in a moment if she were troubled. Tori frowned. She needed an upper hand, needed to gain some control.

"How dare you do this to me." Playing off her earlier displeasure and annoyance about Geoff, she confronted Sally, who stood in front of her on the escalator heading down to the lobby. "You probably knew something like this would happen. What did you say? Something about a break in the routine of life, how life needed spice? Well, if this is the kind of spice you mean, I don't want it. Having a career some women would envy and a stable, or boring as you would call it, relationship is what makes up my perfectly content, comfortable life. Perhaps it needs a little salt, but spice? No."

"Whatever you say, dear." Sally seemed unfazed.

"I should also make it clear to you that, while Mr. McKenzie is working for you, he best stay far away from me…and my life with David."

Sally looked over her shoulder, her eyes narrowed and her lips moved to reply, but she was cut off.

"Ah, why, Sally Becker! Is that you?" A woman called out to them in a painfully bad rendition of a southern drawl.

Victoria and Sally turned in unison to watch the short, ill-dressed women waddle toward them as they debarked the escalator.

"Tweedle Dee and Tweedle Dum," Sally said dryly and only loud enough for Tori to hear.

Tori stifled a snicker and a smile with her hand.

"Mrs. Sims, what a pleasure to see you." Sally's voice oozed bitter pleasantry. "How nice of you to remember me."

"Of course I remember who you are," Gertrude Sims replied, drawing out each word. "If it weren't for your services awhile back, why, my husband's business might have gone belly up. Just like a fish dead out of water." She produced a

&-&-&-&-&-&

sound like chalk scraping on a blackboard. "You know my darling daughter is taking computer science courses. Of course, she doesn't have to since she already has had her degree for several years, but it never hurts to continue learning. Anyhow, perhaps one day you could consider her for a position in your company."

"Perhaps," Sally replied.

Gertrude chortled again.

Her laugh is as hideous as her clothes. Tori's ears hurt hearing the woman talk, and they were downright pained to hear that laugh.

"And who is this fine lady?" Mrs. Sims asked, extending her pudgy little hand toward Tori.

"Me and my manners," Sally said with a rolling sweep of her eyes. "May I introduce my friend and protégé, Ms. Victoria Padden. Victoria, this is Mrs. Gertrude Sims and her daughter, Bertha."

"How do you do?" Tori took Gertrude's hand.

Mrs. Sims lightly grasped her fingertips. "Protégé? How wonderful!"

Speaking of dead fish. Not liking the edge of steel in the woman's voice, Tori smiled pleasantly and out of the corner of her eye caught Bertha's grim-faced expression. The woman stared at her as if she already knew her and hated her. Energetic waves of animosity pulsed from Bertha. The negativity pooled around Tori. A knot formed in her stomach.

"So, Sally," Mrs. Sims continued, "I've noticed you paid a nice sum to retain Mr. McKenzie's services. How long do you intend to work the poor boy?"

The mother's biting coolness sent bolts of alarm through Victoria's veins. She didn't like the two women. Though their light brown hair and pastel color clothing made them look like the fairies from *Sleeping Beauty*, she couldn't help but think they were the evil women from *Cinderella*.

"Our contract is for five weekends."

"Well!" Scraping chalk sounded again. "Don't work him too hard, mind you. We want him in one whole piece when he finally comes around to call on Bertha."

"I'll keep that in mind," Sally's voice lacked amusement.

"Come along, Bertha. Can't keep our driver waiting too much longer." Mrs. Sims took her daughter's hand. "Sally." She nodded. "Victoria, it was a pleasure to make your acquaintance." Gertrude directed her daughter to turn.

The hate-filled stare Bertha threw at her and Sally right before Gertrude escorted her away sent chills down Victoria's spine. *What good could come from being here today? As it stood at the moment…nothing.*

CHAPTER THREE

Journal entry #41

He's met some new ladies. They *bought* him. Paid for his time and attention. Things he could be bestowing on me. That is, if he knew how much I wanted his notice, needed him in my life.

But no. He has no clue.

There have been a few times I've tried to get through to him, but to no avail.

It sucks.

This time though I think I've found a different way to get to him.

Time to put my plans in motion.

CHAPTER FOUR

Come over this afternoon and bring your files. We need to talk.

Sally's stern voice echoed in Victoria's head as she slowly drove up her friend's acre-long, gravel driveway. Her friend had been too business-like in her weekly invitation call for Sunday lunch. Uneasy about what lay in wait, she stopped her black compact car half way up the drive.

After running through her mental checklist and flipping through the top two files on the passenger seat, Tori reassured herself everything was in order. All her work was going smoothly. In fact, some customers had written commendations on how well she had installed their networks. All the systems she controlled were running efficiently and problem free.

"So what is there to discuss?" she asked herself out loud, staring at the house. "And why here?" Business was always conducted at the office.

The brick-faced, center-hall colonial situated upon a lush and manicured lawn, with windows glinting brightly in the afternoon sun, offered her no answers.

Sally had better not have used the accounts as an excuse to get me over here to talk about David. There was nothing to say on that matter. She had arrived home to an empty house late Friday afternoon to find a message stating he had received a last-minute assignment to cover a sick colleague's place at a few seminars in the tri-state area starting in Philadelphia. He wouldn't be back for about a week. The timing of his trip was fortunate. She was still slightly unbalanced from the auction and needed the reprieve. Getting one's desires under control when you had dreamt of a handsome stranger two nights in a row wasn't an easy task.

Tori tapped her fingers on the steering wheel, trying to remember what Sally had said on the way home Friday evening. Was Geoff starting the job at her house this weekend? Or had she said next weekend? For the life of her, she couldn't remember. She had been too wrapped up in her own thoughts about Geoff, those women, and the weird feelings she'd experienced at the hotel to listen to what Sally had said.

She resumed traversing up the drive. The stones crunched loudly under her tires' slow descent. There were no vehicles in sight. That was a good sign. If there were anyone on-site, they'd be parked on the side of the house in front of the garages. Only friends of the family parked in front in the circular section of the drive. Where should she park? Was she a friend or an employee today? This wasn't a normal visit since Sally wanted to talk shop. Then again, business or not, it was Sunday. They were friends. She pulled up to the front.

From the seat beside her, she gathered her stack of folders, got out and slammed the car door with her hip.

For a moment she stood, as she always did when she came over, to take in the view. This is what her parents had wanted for her, what she and David had discussed once one night soon after they had met—buying the big house, a few acres, trees bordering the whole perimeter of the property. Flowerbeds and gardens would dot the grounds. Children would have lots of space to play.

She took a deep breath. The scent of fresh cut grass and flowers mingled in her nose and made her eyes water. The house, land and children were all a dream, though. David was quite content living where he was in Bridgewater in a small house with neighbors who seemed only a foot away in the houses on either side. His home was close to the clinic. He couldn't see making the half hour, or more depending upon traffic, commute from Hunterdon County into work every day. She had to admit she didn't want to drive any farther than she already had to either. And when it came to having children, that discussion had become more taboo than the marriage topic.

Her mother wouldn't be happy to know her daughter wasn't going to have the house, the children, the flowerbed surrounding a small fountain, just like Sally's, maybe not even a doctor for a son-in-law. Then again, David could change and life could turn out different.

Maybe.

With that thought, she went around the car and made her way up the slate steps. The Becker's live-in maid, Ginny, answered her knock on the double doors with a curt hello. The housekeeper had Tori wait in the two-story foyer.

"My, don't we look summery?" Sally commented, coming around the staircase. Wearing a red silk shirt, black dress pants, and her blonde hair pulled back in a perfectly smooth French Twist, she was, as always, the symbol of elegance.

Tori's discomfort deepened seeing her friend's attire. Looking at the pristine white-and-tan marble floor, the sparkling mirrors trimmed in gold and the polished oak banisters of the butterfly staircase, a small wave of homesickness washed over her and she felt out of place. Her worn blue jeans and white tank top covered by a worn jacket seemed to be a blemish on the surroundings. She should have dressed more appropriately. Not to mention her hair. Try as she might to tame her unruly locks back into a thick braid, many strands had escaped, making her look like she had stuck her finger in a light socket. Some days she really hated humidity.

"I'm sorry. I thought since it was Sunday…"

"Don't fret about it." Sally waved her hand, fingers heavily laden with a few large rings. "I shouldn't expect you to be dressed up all the time around me."

ॐॐॐॐॐ

Tori offered a wan smile. *Sure. Don't worry. Easier said than done.*

"Come along into the kitchen. We'll have some lemonade, take a look at those files and talk."

She walked in silence beside her friend, and for the umpteenth time, admired the open floor plan of the house. Every room blended seamlessly into the other. From the grand family room they passed, she could see the back of the staircase, the doors to the library…and usually through an opening in the wall to the kitchen. She had thought it was odd she had been made to wait in the foyer and now wondered at the fact that the kitchen shutters were closed. The reason why sat at the kitchen table.

Halfway into the kitchen, she stopped abruptly and stared at the broad expanse of a man's back. Blood warmed by anger slowly heated her cheeks. Why didn't Sally tell her that man, the haunter of her dreams, the hunk who wouldn't leave her mind, would be here? The rush of desire-laden adrenaline washed anew through her system and reignited the attraction she had fought so hard to subdue all weekend.

At the table, Sally picked up a pitcher of lemonade and refilled Geoff's glass. He looked up to her, flashing a bright smile.

Tori's pulse quickened. Even in profile his smile was disarming.

"Geoff, you remember Victoria, don't you?"

He turned and propped his elbow on the back of the chair. "Yes, I do." His voice was deep and smooth. Sultry. "Nice to see you again, Tori."

The atmosphere, magnetized with his self-confidence and virility, jangled her insides. All she could do was nod in acknowledgement. For a long moment, she studied him. In his dirt-stained jeans and t-shirt, with sweat wetting his hair and beading on his arms, he was the image of a rugged, hardworking Adonis incarnate. Here was a man who wasn't afraid to use his hands, head and body, and get them dirty.

And, man, do I love dirty boys. Or at least I used to in my heyday. Before it got me in trouble.

She thought she detected laughter in his eyes.

Her temper flared once more. She didn't like the situation Sally had put her in, the way his nearness made her head dizzy, or how he seemed to read her thoughts.

"Sally. Outside. Now," she demanded through clenched teeth, then marched out through the open French doors to the brick patio. Breathing deep, she clutched the stack of folders to her chest. Her heart pounded against them.

"I thought Geoff wasn't going to be here for another week," she ranted the moment Sally stepped out and closed the doors behind her, furious with herself and her friend. The warm day did nothing to help cool the fire within her. She had David and a career to deal with and didn't need this reminder of how little control she recently had over her thoughts and physiological reactions to a hot guy. She couldn't afford for her emotions to get battered around, especially since David would notice the difference in her the moment he saw her again. What would she tell him then? "You only contracted him out Friday night. Why didn't you tell me he was going to be here? I thought I told you I didn't want him anywhere near me."

"Calm down, Victoria. Just because he's a handsome, strapping fellow doesn't mean you have to get all flustered." Sally tilted her head and peered at her. "You're blushing. Ah, I see. That's why you don't want him around. *Too male for you?*" She laughed. "I figured why wait on the work. I need it done. He was available immediately, so we started yesterday. He's done a lovely job on the deck, hasn't he?" Sally pointed to the raised deck off the family room. "Remember how the boards were rotting away on the steps? He replaced those. He fixed the foundation, repaired the railing, and put a coat of sealant

on it. Today he's working on the surrounding flowerbed.
What an eye for detail. Told me how the landscaping would
look best, then went to work. See the outlining stones? His
idea. My flowerbed will be the most glorious one in this
neighborhood."

Tori glanced at the spots Sally had pointed to and noticed a
red pickup truck parked on the other side of the deck. Long
pieces of wood hung over the tailgate. Of course, he had
parked in back. Parking close to the job gave easier access to
materials. Why hadn't she thought of that earlier? She sighed.
"Sally?"

"Yes, dear?"

"Wasn't the purpose of this visit to go over my files?" she
asked coolly, hoping to change the subject and let her heated
attitude dissipate.

"Oh, yes, that's right." Sally diverted her attention away
from her flowers and pulled a folder from Tori's vice-like grip.
As she flipped through it, she continued her remarks. "After
he finishes lunch, he's going to put a second coat on the deck.
When he's done, he'll be on his way. Frank finally decided to
do the work himself. Doctor told him it would be good for
him. At least that's what Frank told me. In my opinion, I
believe Frank doesn't like having a good-looking, younger
man around his territory." She closed the file.

"You have his services available for four more weekends,
though." Victoria snatched the file back and shoved another
in Sally's direction, dissuading her body from firing off
anymore sexual pings. She wished her boss would quit
reminding her Geoff was attractive—her comments about
Geoff being virile made shorter, heavy-set David seem less
appealing.

"Yes, I know. That's where you come in."

"What?" Surprised, Tori jerked. The folders jostled, almost
fell out of her arms. She scrambled to right them. "What do
you mean that's where I come in?"

"I'm going to have you become his new employer." Sally closed the second file, gave it back and grabbed two more.

Sally was crazy. Hadn't she heard her saying she didn't want Geoff near her? "I don't have anything for him to do." *Liar.* She had plenty for him to do. Her small house was due for a major overhaul, but she couldn't be around Geoff. Her mind would turn to mush.

"Sure you do." Not looking up as she spoke, Sally perused the fourth file. "David's porch needs repair and he wants half his garage converted to an office, right? Plus, there's always your place, and it does need work since you're never there." Sally exchanged two more files out of Tori's arms. "Just think how David will feel when he finds out he's getting free labor and discounted materials. How is David doing, by the way?"

"He's fine," she replied with a defeated sigh. She couldn't argue with Sally since she was right about the work. She didn't want to argue about David, either.

"What did you two do last night?"

"Well, it turns out he's away for the weekend, so I spent time at my place cleaning. Then I ended up watching television, eating too much Rocky Road and sleeping."

"How exciting," Sally said with perky sarcasm.

"Yeah, very." Victoria sat down on an ironwork bench and placed the folders beside her to relieve her arms.

The hum of an electric edge trimmer at the back edge of the Becker's property caught their attention. A young man glided the contraption around the base of an oak tree. Sally's West Highland terrier ran around the worker and barked at the offensive noise. After a few turns, the dog spun toward the house and tore through the backyard as fast as its little legs could move, heading straight for Victoria.

When he arrived, he jumped into her lap, sniffed her clothing, then licked her face. Squealing with delight, she returned the dog's enthusiasm with a hug and a quick rub on its head.

"Oh, Snowpea, you know better than to jump on people," Sally scolded.

"It doesn't bother me." Tori brushed the dog's hair. "I think it's great. I miss having a dog of my own."

"Still, it's not right for Snowpea to think he can jump on someone. Some visitors don't like it when a dog or any animal lavishes them with any kind of affection." Sally placed the two files on the bench, then clapped. "Snowpea, come down. Come to Momma."

The dog obeyed.

Momma. Victoria smiled. Snowpea, to Frank and Sally, was their child. As her and Sally's friendship grew, she had learned that after many years and attempts to try to conceive, the couple realized they were destined not to have children. As their last straw, they had gone to a fertility specialist. The news was devastating. Sally's body couldn't keep a conception in place. They were both distraught. Sally had taken it hard.

Frank, knowing Sally needed something to fill the void, had brought home a puppy. At first, Sally hadn't taken to the idea. The animal wasn't a child, the baby she so badly wanted. To her, it was just a dog. That same night as she had tried to doze off, she heard the puppy whimper in the kitchen. The sad sound had torn at her soul, so she had gone downstairs, picked up the tiny creature and rocked it to sleep. From that point on, she loved him.

The little white ball of fur she named Snowpea became her pride and joy. Sally admitted she still longed for a baby and wished that part of her life had turned out different. Yet, she wouldn't trade Snowpea for the world. He filled her childless void just enough to make it bearable.

She watched Sally pick up the dog, then focused on the young man. "I've never seen *him* here on the weekend," she commented, concerned about the stranger and perplexed at the heebie-jeebies creeping along her spine again. How long was she going to continue looking at each new person she came across as a threat? She also knew people would call her crazy if she voiced her thoughts about her instincts, so she kept quiet and kept telling herself nothing was going to happen. Hopefully one day she'd start believing that.

"He's new. The service sent him over because Paul's on vacation. Buck, that's the boy's name, is a bit slow-minded, but he's doing a wonderful job."

Buck, who looked like he wasn't more than twenty years of age, turned off his machine and leaned against the oak. He took off his dirty black baseball cap, wiped his forehead with the back of his wrist and looked over at them.

A flashback to the eyes peering through the curtain openings at the auction sent a chill through Tori. Something was off. But what? Her friend was a good judge of character and apparently liked Buck. So why was cold apprehension about the young man weaving its way through her?

She mentally shook off the uneasy sensations, chalking them up again to her own anxieties over what happened in the past.

Sally waved to the groundskeeper. "He's good with mechanical things," she continued. "Fixed the old camping generator Frank had been tinkering with for ages in no time flat. Then when he saw a small oil stain on the driveway, he asked who had a leak. I told him my car was dripping a bit. He said he could fix that, too. Told Frank what he needed, and Frank ran into town to get it." She pet the dog one last time, put him down, and after taking the last two files, scanned them in silence. Finished, she picked up the stack and plopped it down on Victoria's lap. "Well, they all look in order. By the end of this month, you'll have six new accounts. You'll handle fourteen in all including those three major companies we have coming on. How's that sound?"

"Sounds great." Tori relaxed. The chill left her. Finally pleasing news and conversation. Getting more accounts, especially the big ones, equaled a promotion, and this promotion was big. From eight to fourteen. How sweet.

Not quite, her inner voice chided. The business belonged to Frank and Sally. Her associates at CompNet, Incorporated, would think Sally played favorite since she and Sally were friends. Especially Linda Moore. Her co-worker hated the fact she and Sally were close and disliked her even more for it and the *so-called preferential treatment* Sally gave her. It was no secret either Linda wanted those accounts.

"Linda's going to be a problem. She's been working really hard to get these accounts. She already thinks they're hers, and she's going to throw a fit when she hears I have them."

"Pooh on Linda. She has enough to handle. I like the fact she's finally showing some initiative, but her recent motivation is not enough to warrant giving her the accounts. You're getting these accounts based on merit, your hard work," Sally said, sitting down next to Tori. "And having demonstrated success with networking and technical support. I knew when I hired you and began mentorship that you had a talent, so why not reward you? If she raises a stink, send her to me." The older woman patted Tori's leg. "Now, why don't we go back in and join Geoff? We'll have our lunch and you can have some of my famous lemonade. Besides, you'll freckle if you stay out here much longer."

Glancing in through the French doors, Tori observed Geoff's head bow quickly. She'd caught him watching her. He resumed eating.

"Thank you, but no. I have to get back to David's and take care of a few things before he gets home."

"Oh, all right, be that way. I'll tell Geoff to be expecting a call from you."

She slumped her shoulders. Sally hadn't forgotten about pawning Geoff off on her. Tori cringed. She didn't need to be attracted to another man at the moment. Not with the promotion on the way and her separation with David. Then again, he could turn out to be a pretty nice guy under that gorgeous façade of his, and a girl could never have enough friends. "Okay. Fine. Call me, or text me later with his number." Tori stood, brushed the dog fur off her clothes, then picked up her folders. By the time she was done, Sally was back in the house. She caught Geoff gazing at her through the window. This time he made no attempt to hide his apparent appraisal. Startled by his scrutiny, her hand froze on the brass door handle.

Think business, girl. He's only a man. Soon to be your employee. View him as one of your interns.

She released the handle. But none of her interns were so good-looking. A tickle of pleasure played in her stomach. She forced the sensation away. Business was business with no room for pleasure and her business here was through.

Without going in to say goodbye, she noted where Buck continued to trim the lawn, turned and hurried in the opposite direction around the outside of the house to her car.

* * * *

Geoff downed the rest of his lemonade and continued to gaze through the windows even though Tori was no longer there to look at. The weekend had been grueling and working outside in mid-September was still quite warm. Around one o'clock when Sally had halted his work, telling him to come inside for lunch, he obliged willingly.

At least the work helped cover his disappointment. Against his better judgment, he'd hoped to see Victoria. He wanted to see if she was as pretty as his dreams remembered her to be. And, a small part of him wanted to ask her out. Yet, as the morning wore on, he realized not seeing her was for the best. He didn't need the distraction of a woman or the problems involvement with one would cause. At this point, a new relationship wouldn't be a wise choice for his business or his life.

Yet, just as he got his mind back on track, she had come in.

Everything took on a clean brightness when he saw her, and she was as beautiful as he remembered. Her hair, pulled back from her face in a braid with a gold barrette, showed off the dusty rose of her cheeks. She looked so fresh and appealing in her white tank top and tight fitting jeans, he wished he could have cleaned up and not felt so grimy. In the end, though, her arriving and his feelings hadn't mattered. In her arms were a stack of folders, and needing to talk to Sally, they had gone out to the patio, leaving him to his meal.

He had had a clear view of them through the windows and was able to observe her as they exchanged the files and talked.

She had appeared as business-minded as he was. Both of them were working on a Sunday. He didn't know many women who would do that. Then again he didn't know many women period. Who knew what females did or didn't do on the weekends anymore? He sighed. Maybe a relationship with someone like Tori wouldn't be complicated. Maybe being involved with her would be worth it.

His level of attraction for her was deep. Her inviting lush full lips wanted to be kissed, her body touched. Musing to the point of realizing a cold shower was in order, Geoff shook his head to change his thoughts. He took a deep breath.

A woman like her would understand his drive to succeed, his late hours and long work weeks, and wouldn't be frightened off by his passion for his livelihood. Then again, who was he kidding? None of the women he had ever been with stuck around, business-minded or not. Even his wife.

"Some more lemonade, Geoff?" Sally inquired, stirring him from his introspection.

"Yes, thank you."

"Would you like some strawberry shortcake? I made it this morning."

"Yes, please."

She prepared a plate and placed it before him on the table.

"Thank you Mrs. Bec... Sally. It's very kind of you to make me lunch. You didn't have to go to all the trouble."

"No bother at all." She took a seat across from him and watched him eat. "I enjoy cooking. I also enjoy seeing a man with a healthy appetite."

Had he heard a seductive undertone in her last statement? Were those men at the auction right? That wealthy women wanted... A rush of blood warmed his face.

"There's nothing to be ashamed about, Geoff. You're a big man. You need to eat. Have to satisfy your *desires*."

He nodded, unable to speak. He popped a piece of cake in his mouth, then another. He kept his gaze down. How did a man deal with a woman of her position when she was so bold?

"Victoria's a nice young lady, isn't she?"

His head shot up. The cake stuck in his throat. So that was it. Sally played the other role—the matchmaking momma. He was relieved she wasn't coming on to him, but were his thoughts about Tori that obvious? After getting the food down, he composed his voice as best he could. "From what I gather, she is."

Granted, he only had her looks to go by, so it wasn't a total lie. She was very appealing, especially when the sunlight played in her hair. The fiery gold and copper highlights in her brown locks burned in his memory. He'd wished he could stop work and just watch her for the rest of the afternoon. As for her personality, though, he couldn't tell. Both times she had been near him, she had been stunned into silence. She had come in with barely a hello and left just as fast without a goodbye.

"Then you won't mind finishing out your contract with her."

"What?" He dropped the fork. The utensil clattered loudly on the plate.

"I'm subcontracting you out. She'll be giving you a call to discuss the details. Probably will have you start on her boyfriend's—" Sally coughed over the word. "House."

"Boyfriend?" He tried to sound casual, but his voice hitched. *Just my luck.* He should have known a pretty woman like her would be attached. Her involvement with another was for the best anyway. As he had decided before, he couldn't afford to get involved and have his feelings for a woman muck up his life.

"Don't look so grim, Geoff. It's not serious. In fact, they're in the midst of a trial separation. Just go and do a good job on—for Tori."

Geoff halfheartedly agreed to her request. Whether he liked the thought of working for Tori or not, he had to. He was under contract and business was business no matter how he looked at the situation.

"Lovely." Sally's eyes glittered.

Yeah, lovely. Just lovely. First the Simses and now Sally. *I should have become a priest.*

CHAPTER FIVE

*T*ori stared at the piece of David's stationary in her hand. The letter he'd written, and left on the kitchen table for her to find, served as a reminder why they were on a break, made her see just how much the past week had been so pleasant, too. With him not around, she felt free to be herself, to be unguarded. He'd never know about her rollercoaster state of emotions—the warmth that continually flushed her face, her daydreaming, or her goose pimpled flesh. All because she couldn't stop thinking of a certain handsome man in a tight pair of jeans nor the freaky people she'd come across. She'd even slept at David's a couple of times to keep her anxiety levels low. Her house was great, but it sat way off a road in a lightly populated area. At least at David's, if something were to happen, there were neighbors a foot or two away. They'd be able to hear her scream, help her…unlike last time.

The paper crunched in her hand rousing her from the terrible thoughts. No more staying at his house. She'd have to pull up her big girl panties and make the best of things at her own place from now on.

And all she had wanted to do was surprise David. The way she'd figured it, if she did something nice for him, maybe it'd open the lines of communication again. *Well, it sure had. Just not in the way I had hoped.*

Calling Geoff had taken her three days due to the need to gather her courage, but she had. To her surprise, Geoff had agreed to help her with her idea for David's house. And, this time forewarned was forearmed. She practiced the relaxation and meditation techniques David had taught her to calm her mind, body and spirit, and to focus her control. She had vowed when she was in the presence of that unnerving man, her mind would maintain its faculties.

What a fool I was.

She shouldn't have worried about her reaction to Geoff. She should have worried more about David's.

A vivid recollection of the previous night's fight flooded her mind. David had come home, seen the work in progress in the garage and had demanded an explanation. Breaking down under his interrogation, she had told him all about the auction, *sans* feelings for Geoff, and her idea to begin the renovations for his home office.

"What were you thinking, Victoria?" David had screamed, running his short fingers through his mousy brown hair. "How could you conceive to interrupt *my* life, take over *my* house, like this?"

"You've talked about converting the garage into useful space for a year now and how you need to take action on the project. I thought the surprise, my getting the ball rolling for you, would be nice."

"Surprise me you did!" His pale brown eyes had glared furiously at her. "Coming home to find a mess and an alteration in my routine, after a week of travels, was very unsettling. Plus the thought of you alone, here, with another man was nerve-racking."

"I wasn't even here. I was called into work before he arrived, so I left him instructions and a key. Nothing happened."

"You left a perfect stranger a key to my house?" David's small mouth snapped shut and became a thin white line before he sharply exhaled. "My God, Victoria, I thought you were smarter than that."

She'd winced at the remark. She *was* intelligent. Having graduated in the top ten in high school and the top fifth in college, she didn't like when anyone implied she was dumb. Anger had boiled within her.

"Do you find anything missing?" she had asked very slowly and quietly, sweeping her arm out to encompass the room. "No, of course not. Why would Geoff want to ruin his reputation? And, as I just said, he's not a perfect stranger. Sally hired him at the auction, and he spent all last weekend with her. I trust her judgment. She wouldn't refer a criminal to us."

His round face had grown red and swollen. She'd expected it to burst.

"That brings me to another point," David seethed. "I'd prefer it if you didn't see Sally anymore. She's not a good influence on you."

Blown away by his command and blinded by her fury, she hadn't caught David's retreat from the living room.

"That's preposterous," she'd shouted at the footsteps above her when she'd noticed his absence. "She's my boss, you idiot."

David hadn't talked to her the rest of the night though she kept trying to communicate. Then fearing the drive home so late at night, she'd stayed in the guest room, hoping in the morning David would see the situation in a better light.

But he wasn't even around. When the sound of hammering outside woke her, she had gone downstairs to find him and rationally continue the discussion from the night before. Instead, she'd found his letter in the kitchen. She clutched the paper.

All she'd wanted to do was help him. What thanks had she gotten? None. Just a nasty little letter stating even though he appreciated her concern and assistance in the matter of household repairs and getting his office ready, she was not to hire anyone or do anything anymore without his prior approval. He had also requested she fire the current help or have him desist from work until he arrived home. His unreadable signature flared at the bottom.

No *Love*, no *Yours*, not even a *Sincerely* or *Friend* signed off the note. There was only his name. Wasn't that the norm for him, though? He never put anything at the bottom of his missives. He claimed closings at the end of letters tended to raise false expectations.

She had never understood what he had meant until now. If he had put *Love* at the bottom of one note one day then *Yours* at the bottom of another on a different day, she might have assumed something was wrong when there wasn't. Or vice versa, using *Yours* then *Love*, she would have believed everything was great when there could have been something wrong.

His house. His life. His. His. His. Guess it hadn't mattered that she paid part of the water and electric bills because she used the services when she was in the house. She paid part of the phone bill because she made business phone calls, and she paid part of the food bill because she ate. But according to him she gave nothing, didn't support the household. He paid the mortgage, the insurance, the taxes and the upkeep.

In short, he made the rules.

A stirring of guilt settled in Tori's stomach. She hated lies, and she had lied when she had told Sally they rarely ever fought. When it came down to it, everything between her and David was a battle of wills, a fight for control. Yet, if she had told Sally the truth, the news would have added more fuel to her friend's quest *To Rid Tori of David*.

A heated curse outside the kitchen window startled her.

She patted the dampness from her cheeks. To have Geoff see her crying wouldn't do. Tracing the words of David's note with her fingertips, the warmth of new tears brimmed in her eyes. She lifted her head to fight them back. Through her watery vision, a framed photograph on the wall in front of her melted into view. The picture of a happy couple stared back.

It was one of her favorites of her and David, taken at a summer concert down in Holmdel. They had general seating on the hill, treated the evening like a picnic under the stars. Back then at the beginning of their relationship, being with David was ideal. Their relationship had been so ordered and controlled. No risks involved. Steady as a rock. They were good together.

If only all that were true. The tears which she had been holding in check flooded back. She put her head down on her arms on the kitchen table.

The back door creaked on its hinges. Startled, Tori turned toward the sound. Geoff stood in the opening. Sweat beaded and trickled down the well-sculpted and tanned muscles of his shirtless torso. His flat stomach was exactly how she had pictured it would be. The sunlight cast a beautiful glow on him. She wondered if the other parts of him would be like she imagined. Warmth flooded her wet cheeks and spread throughout her body. She offered a tentative smile.

"Excuse me, Miss Padden. Didn't mean to disturb you." He walked into the room, his concerned-filled gaze quickly raking over her then landing on the floor. "I just came in for drink. You would think it's still summer with how hot it's getting out there."

"It's okay," she said getting up and taking a few wobbly steps over to the counter. "Water, iced tea, soda?"

"Water will do just fine."

She pulled a glass out of the cabinet. Her hands shook as she turned on the faucet and held the glass underneath the tap. The force of the faucet's pressure splashed water on her shirt. Silently, she said a prayer of thanks she'd worn sweats and a t-shirt to bed and not her usual flimsy nightgown. Movement outside the window above the sink caught her attention, sent shivers through her. With a silent curse at her jumpiness, she watched a cardinal hop across the lawn, then take flight to an awaiting tree branch.

Flight. She wished she could fly away from her troubles. What a morning this had turned out to be. Waking up late to periodic banging. Reading a letter that was cementing her and David's separation. Thinking about a hot guy and then encountering said handsome, shirtless man in her ex-boyfriend's house. And she had yet to have her morning cup of coffee.

She was going to lay into Sally the next time she saw her.

"Umm, Miss Padden?"

Tori jerked her gaze away from the window to the water running out of the glass and over her fingers. With a quick dip, she dumped out the excess and spun to deliver the drink. The glass slipped out of her hand. In a confident move, Geoff was at her side and caught the container inches from the floor. More water sloshed out. Dumbfounded, she looked down at the puddle.

He placed the glass on the counter, grabbed a dish towel and tossed it onto the wet spot. Then he took her chin in his hand, tilted up her face. "Are you all right? You look like you're upset over something more than spilt water."

She lowered her gaze and shrugged.

"Here." He ripped a paper towel off the hanging roll next to the window and gave it to her.

She gently blotted her eyes and nose. Why did she have to meet such a nice guy like him now? Why couldn't it have happened two years ago? Happened before she met David? New tears wet her lashes.

"Come now. It can't be that bad."

She shrugged her shoulders again, not speaking for fear of what her voice would reveal.

Without asking, he wrapped gentle arms around her.

Like a little girl in need of affection, she settled into his outstretched arms and kept her hands near her face to use the towel for her sniffles. His embrace tightened.

A gleam of understanding flickered in her mind. This was what she had been missing. Real affection, given freely and spontaneously. Care and friendliness that didn't expect anything in return. She had never had tenderness in her wild days, and she sure didn't have it with David.

Needing to feel another's strength, to have the force permeate her and make her strong again, she traced her hands up the smooth, hard contours of his chest. When they reached the back of his neck, she let the towel drop and laced her fingers together.

She took a deep breath. His skin smelled of coconuts and sun. Not caring about the dampness of his body, she nuzzled her cheek against his soft skin and listened to the steady beat of his heart. His solid body tensed, then relaxed beneath her.

Too bad they couldn't stay this way forever.

"Feeling better?"

Tori nodded, rubbing her cheek gently on his chest, thinking about her daydreams, and wanting to run the tips of her fingers over his chest.

"Let me see." He pulled away, tilted up her chin again and looked into her eyes. "How about a smile?"

She complied. He was sweet to care in the first place.

"I don't see why such a beautiful lady would ever have cause to cry. It's a shame you should."

"Thank you," she said softly, shocked by the compliment.

"No need to thank me for something that's true."

Searching his warm, brown eyes, she waited for a punch line. None came. A shadow from some clouds drifted past the kitchen window and a sunbeam filtered through. A soft, sensuous light illuminated them. Geoff shifted. His face came within an inch from hers. Tori gazed deeper into his beautiful eyes, finding them flecked with gold and sending out a silent invitation. Slowly, seductively her gaze slid downwards and appraised his full, luscious lips.

Before she could take her next breath, his mouth descended on hers. A brief moment of shock stiffened her body then, as if they had always been intimate, she relaxed and molded against him. His mouth sensuously moved upon hers, and when his lips parted, she followed suit.

His tongue searched her mouth. With a newfound hunger she matched his movements and ran her fingers through his soft hair reveling in the locks' silkiness. Happiness and desire, combined with a feeling of forbidden pleasure, created a stormy sea of sensation in her middle. Her toes curled. She was lost and found in his kiss. She was safe. She was secure. And, she believed, desired. She smoothed her hands down the tops of his shoulders and upper arms to his chest. Doing what she had dreamt of and yearned to do minutes before, she smoothed her fingers over his chest.

Geoff moaned into her mouth.

Outside a car door slammed.

"David's home," she murmured as if lost in pleasant dream. Tori abruptly pulled out of Geoff's embrace and pushed him away. "David!" She glanced at the stove's clock. Eleven forty-five. Where had the morning gone? "Oh, no."

"What is it?"

"You have to go. Get back outside. Clean up the porch. There won't be an office." She sounded frantic, idiotic. But what did she expect after a kiss like that? "Oh, God."

David's footsteps grew louder on the gravel outside. There was no time to think about what just happened. She ran from the room to go put on some clothes.

* * * *

Bewildered by her actions during the kiss, the display of emotions that had played across her face and her swift departure, Geoff picked up the glass of water, went to the table and glanced down at the letter. From his scan of the paper, it all became clear to him—the reason for her tears and flight from the room. There were problems between her and David, and he'd just added to them by kissing her.

David's arrival echoed on the back porch.

No need for me to cause any more trouble. He left the letter where it lay to meet David at the door.

"Morning, Mr. Lloyd."

"Morning, Mr. McKenzie. I take it you are well."

"Yes, I am." Geoff nonchalantly ran his fingers through his hair to comb it back in place.

"I hope I'm assuming correctly that Victoria has spoken with you?"

"Yes, she has. I'm to clean off the porch and there won't be an office." Geoff downed the water, watched David cross the kitchen floor, and put his briefcase on top of the tear-stained letter. He placed the glass on the counter.

"Actually, there will be an office, but it won't be done by you. I'm having my own contractors come in to do the work next weekend. I'll make sure Victoria sends you what you're due."

"It's been a pleasure," Geoff replied through clenched jaws. David's contemptuous tone sparked his anger, and on his way out, he made sure to slam the door behind him.

* * * *

Tori, listening to the exchange from the top of the stairs, winced at David's attitude. Sally was right. He was a prick. How could he be a healer of minds and souls when he had such a great knack of making people miserable? *Look at what he's done to me.* She hugged her body against her knees.

It was time to move back to her house for good, give them each more time to assess their feelings, to make sure being with each other was right. She'd have to buy and install some motion-detector lights, maybe an alarm system, to make herself feel safe, but that was all right.

Her spirits lifted. The decision felt right, really right. In the guest room, she changed into jeans and a blouse, pulled out her suitcase and packed her remaining garments. In the bathroom, she rushed to retrieve the rest of her personals. After throwing everything into the bag in a haphazard manner, she placed it near the bedroom door and went in to make the bed.

"Good morning, Victoria."

"Hello, David," she said with a quick glance, wondering how she had missed hearing his heavy footsteps.

"Is something wrong?" He came in uninvited and sat down creasing the sheets she had straightened. "Something seems to be bothering you."

"Nothing's bothering me." *Has he already forgotten the note he left me? The fight we had?* She stiffly turned away and went to the other side of the bed.

"Fine. If you don't want to discuss it right now…"

She grinned to herself. The pause, his technique of leaving an opening so she would fill it, was so characteristic of his psychobabble. She wouldn't give him the satisfaction of analysis. Not this time.

"Okay, fine. You don't want to talk. You want to mope, but this should cheer you. I've decided to schedule some time with you today."

"How nice of you, David." Sarcasm dripped from her voice. She was so tired of his exacting ways.

"I thought we could spend some quality time together," he said, laying down on his side and patting the bed.

She opened her mouth to tell him he could spend the time petting himself, but snapped it shut, and instead yanked the sheet under him. After she re-straightened and tucked the material under the mattress, she placed her hands on her hips and glared at him.

"Not today, David." *Three weeks of nothing, not even a kiss, and of all days,* today *he wants to be romantic.* "I have things I need to do." She picked up and beat one of the pillows.

"Really? What would those things be?"

"I'm going home." She glanced at the bag near the door.

His gaze followed suit. "To Albany for a few days? You should have told me. I would have made arrangements to come with you." He shrugged. "Well, too late now. Tell your parents I said hello."

"No. I'm going to *my* home. Remember? I have my own place. I moved back there when we decided to cool things."

"Oh. Yes. That's right. You're having issues with what I do or don't do. What I say or don't say. And the letter I left probably hasn't helped your attitude any. You know how picky I get. I like everything to be just right."

The false humbleness in his voice infuriated her more. "Yeah, I know." Her voice was a whisper and edged with steel. She went to the door and grabbed her bag.

"What's that tone for?"

"You're the shrink, *Doctor* David. You figure it out." She turned her back on him, grabbed her suitcase and left.

Tori heard him growling as she descended the stairs. She couldn't believe she had called him the two things he hated most in the world—shrink because he said it's degrading, and Doctor because he still had his dissertation to do to get the title.

Let him stew.

On her flight through the kitchen, she pulled the photograph off the wall and stuck it in the trash. Nothing else of hers remained in the house. No trace remained to indicate she'd ever lived there. It was as if she had never existed in David's life, and as of that moment, that was exactly the way she wanted it.

CHAPTER SIX

*V*ictoria entered her home, placed her briefcase on the coffee table and collapsed onto the sofa. The clock on the combination DVD/VCR unit ticked the seconds away beneath three tiny letters *MON*. She stared at the pale blue display. It seemed like an eternity had passed since she had left David's for good, yet the time elapsed had only been one day. She couldn't believe David hadn't called her. They never went more than a day without speaking, whether in person or on the phone. A bitter taste filled her mouth. Who was she kidding? A whole month had gone by and they had barely spoken to each other.

She pried herself from off the couch. She and David had to talk, and though it pained her to be the one to break down and make the first move, she would call him. In her home office, she released her French Twist and shook out her hair to alleviate the throbbing in her temples. She hit the speed dial button for his number.

"Hello?"

The warm, comforting voice on the other end of the line startled her. After a brief moment, she remembered she had rearranged her speed dial during a wine-induced moment where she needed to change everything connected to her ex. David no longer had the place of honor at number one and her parents now did. Too bad she hadn't been lucid enough to re-label the numbers. Who knew who had which speed dial number now.

"Hi, Mom."

"Why, darling, what a surprise. How are you doing? Is everything all right?"

Tori took a deep breath, related the events of the past several days and smiled at her mother's gasp of delight when she told her about the auction. She had been right, her mother was very happy to hear about it. Spurred on by the news, Mrs. Padden reminisced about her debut into society and meeting her husband at a ball.

Before her mother could get anymore carried away with stories she had already heard a thousand times, Tori interrupted her and informed her of the aftermath. "So you see, Mom, this event did nothing to help my standing in society. If anything, my tiny progress was harmed because I don't think I'll become a doctor's wife after all." She wondered for a moment if she should have included the cold attitudes of the Simses, what had transpired between her and Geoff, and the weird feelings she'd been experiencing about people, but she didn't. She hadn't come to any conclusions when it came to those women who could easily alienate her from society, David, Geoff or her hyper-sensitive instincts. Plus, she didn't believe her mom would understand any of it.

"Oh, sweetheart, it was only a spat. It's natural for them to happen in a relationship. Even your father and I argue at times. David means well. You have to remember a doctor's life is very demanding. Just keep your chin up and be the best woman a man can have."

After several more minutes of her mother's lamentations on the news of her return to her house and her promotion, Victoria said her goodbye and hung up the phone, dissatisfied.

What had she expected? That her mom would say dump David and move on? Her mom was thrilled her daughter was in a relationship with a soon-to-be doctor, and when it came to feeling like a slave and having fights, it was a part of life. Mrs. Padden, the prime example of how a wife of a man of influence should be, hadn't worked for anyone except her family and had volunteered her time and efforts for any social event that would promote her husband's standing. Felicia Padden had paid her dues and now was able to relax and enjoy the benefits of being rich. In time, her mom had said, she would know that luxury, too.

Perhaps, but she knew her and David's relationship was quite different than her parents' in many important aspects. Where her parents were openly affectionate and loving with each other, she and David were remote. Maybe in time that would change. Maybe it wouldn't.

At the doorway of her office Tori scanned her small living room. It had seemed like forever since she had moved out of this little house. Yet it really hadn't been any time at all in the scheme of things.

The monstrous desk, her computer equipment and accessories sat in the room behind her, and she was surprisingly glad the items hadn't been transferred. She'd been waiting for David to say she could move her furniture over. Big and small pieces that still sat where she had first placed them five years ago. But David hadn't like her worn, homey-looking amenities. He'd said he didn't want the eyesores in his house. It was as if he had known she wouldn't be a permanent resident.

The furnishings were too heavy and bulky to have been carted back and forth, anyway. She was also thankful she'd had enough sense to keep the utilities on and paid. Maybe, deep down, she, too, had known she wasn't long for David's place.

Enough, she told herself. If David didn't want to call and talk to her, then she didn't want to speak to him, either. Two could play at that game. Besides, Sally had given her two new accounts which would immerse her in work, and she had a house to fix up. Those chores would definitely help keep her mind occupied and off her crumbled relationship.

Taking a moment to breathe and enjoy the silence, she closed her eyes. A slight breeze blew in through the open window of her office, followed by the growing sound of a mechanic growl and rumble. The reverberation of a motorcycle nearing her property instilled terror in her.

A loud pop and crack from the bike occurred close to her property. Tori jumped, clutching the staccato pulsing at her throat and hating the creepy crawly sensations prickling her skin. Memories of an old relationship gone bad clawed at the forefront of her mind, but she pushed them back down to the dark recesses, locked them in the memory boxes for examination at a later date. It was a visit down a lane she didn't want at the moment.

The breeze kicked up a notch. Something scraped on the surface of her house. Flinching at the noises, she cursed her frayed nerves with a heavy sigh. Her fear of motorcycles and strangers was out of hand. Here she was safe and sound inside, and all she wanted to do was run and hide.

Nothing's going to happen to me. No one's out to get me. I need to let the past rest and focus on my future. And there's been at least one stranger recently who hasn't set my alarm bells ringing.

As much as she hated to do it, she turned off her cell phone. She was physically exhausted, mentally drained, and didn't need her evening at home delegated out to clients. *Not like they would be left in a lurch.* They could call in and speak with someone in the call center if they had trouble. Back at the couch, she opened her briefcase and pulled out a magazine she had bought on the way home. *Home Design.* The shiny cover alluded to decorating and updating while on a budget.

Planning the renovation of her house was what she needed to do to clear her head and refocus. The project would help her feel in control and keep her mind occupied, thus letting her subconscious work out the kinks in her problems. She smiled at the logic of it and pulled out a notebook, pen and

෨ඁ෨ඁ෨ඁ෨ඁ

calculator to jot down her ideas. Half an hour later, she read over her list and the approximate costs. The excitement that had been ballooning over her plans burst. She'd be able to do what she wanted, except the renovation would take her forever to do it all by herself. Especially when it came to the complex projects, like the deck she wanted to build onto the back of her house. She could handle a paint brush and do a mediocre job with wallpaper. Give her a hammer and some nails, however, and she was all thumbs. She had to admit, though, the thought of painting wasn't all that fun either.

If only Geoff were around. With his help she'd have her home fixed up in no time. She smiled at the possibility of seeing him again, talking to him and listening to his smooth voice. *Maybe another kiss?*

No. She couldn't call him. Not after what happened the other day. How could she hire him? Anyway, he was probably sore about being let off the job at David's. Not that he should be. It wasn't like he was being paid for the work.

What had happened in the kitchen? Yes, it was nice having affection lavished on her. Yes, it was nice to feel desired. Her soul, unfettered by the kiss, sang in its freedom, its reawakened passion. He had unleashed a dormant yearning in her to feel needed as a woman. Several years ago, party-girl she was, she would have thrown caution to the wind and had some fun with him regardless of the ramifications. But could she have someone working in her home who had the ability of bringing that out in her?

She did need assistance with her house, though, and he was more than capable to lend a hand. After a bit of thought, she determined his being near her would be all business, no pleasure. She would make a set of rules. Rule number one, no kissing. Enjoyable or not, she couldn't allow those kind of liberties to be taken again until other aspects of her life were straightened out.

Tori snatched her smartphone out of her briefcase, pulled up Geoff's number and hit dial, planning to give him five rings to pick up.

A husky male voice answered on the fourth.

"Geoff McKenzie?"

"Yes?" His voice was hesitant.

"Hi. It's Victoria Padden."

"Why, Ms. Padden, what a pleasure. How can I be of service?"

She tucked the phone between her head and shoulder to free her hands and nervously rearranged some papers within her briefcase.

"Well...I wanted to...to apologize for yesterday. And...and I'd like to hire your services again." She clamped her teeth together. Why couldn't her mouth work right when she talked to him?

There was a loud expulsion of air on the other end. "Thanks, but no thanks. I'm not going to work for that guy again."

"David?"

"Yeah."

A deep silence crossed over the line while Tori digested his attitude. "I'm sorry about how he was with you," she replied in a quiet voice, embarrassed Geoff had been subjugated to David's holier-than-thou attitude. "But it's not for him. It's for me and my place."

"Don't you live with that creep, though? Aren't you his?"

Tori huffed. What was it about men and their cranky, cocky attitudes? "Number one, David is not a creep. He's just...just..." Try as she might, she couldn't come up with something nice to say. "He's just David. And number two, if you knew I was *his*, as you so nicely put it, then why'd you kiss me?"

Only silence answered.

"Do you want the job or not?" Tori asked, frustrated with the conversation and herself for letting him get the best of her.

There was only more silence. She dreaded the thought of having to interview other contractors. Men who believed they could take advantage of females and whose stomachs and backsides were known to hang out of their clothes. Grimacing with the thought, she vowed she'd do the work herself before she hired anyone else.

"I'll pay you for your help," she added boldly, in one last attempt to gain his service.

"Pay me?"

"That's what I said." What was with this guy? Of course the subject of money would raise him from his stupor, but to be caustic then incredulous? "Look, I don't have the time or the patience to interview others. I'm busy with my own contracts. Yet my grandmother's place, which was left to me upon her passing, is crying out for help. Put your feelings for David aside. Are you in or not?" There. Everything was out on the table. It was his turn to lead. If he said no, she would break down and learn how to do the renovations on her own. It would take her months, perhaps forever, to do them, but flying solo would be better than hiring some overweight clod showing ass crack.

"Victoria?"

"Yes?"

"You don't have to pay me. At least not yet. There's still three weekends left according to the charity contract. If there's work remaining to be done after it's up, we'll sit down and arrange other terms then."

"Good." Happiness lilted her voice while relief flooded her system. "Can you be here around eight in the morning on Saturday?"

"Hold on a sec."

There were two echoing thumps followed by muffled footsteps, and after a few moments, the silence was interrupted by the ruffling and snapping of paper. An image of Paul Bunyon using a tiny day planner popped into her head. She stifled a giggle.

"That will be fine. Oh, and Victoria, promise me one thing."

"Yes?"

"Make sure that guy stays away, because if he does come around, the work will stop and I *will* walk."

"I don't think that'll be a problem."

"Great. It's a deal then. See you Saturday."

* * * *

Geoff stared at the black cordless phone lying silent on his glass coffee table. What the hell was he thinking? Had he lost his mind? Trance-like, he rose from his couch, went to the kitchen and grabbed a beer from the refrigerator. In a few swift gulps, he finished it. He pulled out another.

Back in the living room he stared into his fireplace. The dusty embers from last season's fires, all two of them, piled under the grate. He barely saw them. All he could see was the woman he had recently met. Victoria Padden.

She had plagued his thoughts and dreams. Images of them together, clothed and unclothed, had popped into his head at the most inopportune times and had interfered with his work. Though, bothersome as the scintillating images might have been, he welcomed them every time Mrs. Sims called.

That society matron was a pain in his ass, calling to see if he was well, if he wasn't being worked too hard, if he was going to ask Bertha out soon. It was getting to the point that he felt like he was being stalked. The woman, and sometimes with her daughter in tow, seemed to be everywhere he was, knew his schedule sometimes better than himself. He wanted to bellow, "Get a clue! Get a life!" He would never get near her daughter, let alone date her.

ৡৰ৽ৡৰ৽ৡৰ৽

But he could never bring himself to say those things. His common sense prevailed and helped him to keep refusing politely. It was the same sentence, paraphrased every time so he wouldn't sound like a broken record, "Mrs. Sims, I'm sorry. I'm a very busy man right now and your daughter deserves someone who would be able to give her attention and affection. She doesn't need someone she would never see."

Placated, Gertrude would agree and tell him he was very kind to be so considerate of her darling Bertha's feelings. Then, like clockwork, a few days later she would call again.

It bothered him to no end how he had to be respectful and couldn't put the woman in her place, but her husband owned and operated one of the buildings Geoff's company continued to landscape and maintain. Mr. Sims was one of his three biggest and best accounts. There was no doubt in his mind one wrong word to Mrs. Sims and she'd go tell him and the man would pull his business away.

Having met Victoria, though, he found keeping his tongue in check was easier than ever. All he had to do was picture her and his mind softened. The distraction helped most when he could hear Bertha's disturbed crying in the background. What was with women and their crying? His mom's crying. His ex-wife's crying. Bertha's crying. Tori's crying.

His groin stiffened with the memory of Tori's body pressed against his. He shifted his position on the black leather couch. His hug, a force of habit, had been a mistake. His body knew the difference between comforting his mother and comforting a young, attractive woman. He couldn't help the overwhelming desire that had built in him. He couldn't stop himself from kissing her.

Fate through its fortunate wisdom had interrupted a bad situation from getting worse. *That man* had come home. Tori had fled. He had been left to his own defenses, which had given him enough time to read the letter on the table and let his ardor cool.

᠅᠊᠊᠊᠅᠊᠊᠊᠅

Tori seemed to be a pleasant person. Her significant other, however, was a different story.

What an ass to treat a woman the way he did. In their brief exchange, Geoff understood why Victoria was so upset. Remembering the tears she had shed and thinking about her situation pulled at his heartstrings. He didn't like the feeling.

He shouldn't get involved. But, if that was the case, then why was he going back to her?

Because he wanted to see her, plain and simple. He couldn't reason not seeing her ever again, especially after that kiss. He wanted to get to know her, see where a relationship would lead, and for some reason, he wanted to show her there was more to life.

What if she's happy with her life the way it is?

Geoff shook his head and drained the remainder of his beer. That wasn't plausible. If she was content she wouldn't have been crying, nor have responded to him the way she did. She had yielded so easily to him, her soft lips pliant and sweet. It had been a long time since he had enjoyed such a reaction. His lips and chest burned from remembering her touches.

Careful, boy. Remember the last time you were tempted by a woman. What if there's another situation and she goes all strange on you? He emitted a shaky laugh. His inner voice was usually, if not always, right. In his world, relationships inevitably led to trouble. Yet, he wanted to pursue one with Tori, and deep in his bones, he knew he was heading straight toward a huge hassle. But he couldn't stop.

CHAPTER SEVEN

"As you can see, this house needs a lot of work." Tori sat down at a small, unfinished-oak kitchen table after giving Geoff a tour of her small home.

"You aren't kidding." He glanced at the floor covered in a light orange linoleum and the cabinets made of dark brown paneling. "The avocado-colored major appliances are way beyond their prime. So's the green shag carpets and light mint-colored walls. And don't get me started on the bathroom with its bright neon-colored, large, floral designed wall paper. It assaulted my vision," he said with a laugh, dragging in a breath of her clean, fresh scent. "You poor thing. You live in a time warp." Geoff pulled out a chair, turned and straddled it with a smile. A lot of work would mean a lot of time to spend with her. "The whole place needs an overhaul."

At his bemused tone, Tori drew her attention away from her notes and gazed at him. A muscle quivered in his jaw as he held back a laugh. He didn't want her to think he was making fun of her tastes.

A slow, deep exhale escaped her. "It's true. The bathroom looks horrible, and the decor isn't what I'd have chosen for such a small room, but my grandmother put the wallpaper up herself and had worked hard to make this house her own."

"Grandmother? Don't you live here alone?"

Tori nodded. "My grandparents used to live here. After my father and aunt were grown and on their own, Grandma and Pop wanted a smaller house so they bought this one. This place used to be a guest house on the property of that big house just beyond the trees closer to the main road. Eight years ago when Pop died, Grandma decided to stay here. She passed on five years after him and left the house to me. It hasn't been updated in thirty some years."

"That's for sure." He chuckled.

"And, just so you know, I have a very plain, light beige wallpaper and seashell design border for the bathroom. My notes for the rest of the house are in here."

"Good. I like a woman with a plan," he said, pushing up on the back of the chair and standing. "Let's say we put your ideas into action and get started."

She had forgotten about plastic covers for the furniture, but he'd come to the rescue by retrieving sheets from his truck. After he moved the bedroom furniture away from the walls, he took off his shirt and replaced it with a cheap t-shirt he bought. Then, from her closet, she had pulled out some old bed linens, and at his direction, had covered the floor. They had taken their time cleaning and preparing the bedroom walls with primer, and a few hours later, they took a short break. Now they stood back, looking at the walls and the plastic-covered mound in the center of the room.

"The primer's gonna have to dry overnight." His statement was almost lost in the overwhelming noise coming in through the open windows of a motorcycle careening down the road. It was strange any riders would choose to travel the road Tori's house was on. When he rode, he tried to avoid certain streets due to an overage of ruts and bumps and potholes. Tori's road was littered with all three. He glanced at her. Tori's face had gone pale. Her arm hung limp at her side, the brush barely staying in her hand. "Tori? You okay?"

Another motorcycle sped by again outside. She jumped. Paint splattered onto her leg and floor. "The same pop and crack…" she muttered.

"Tori?"

Her gaze fell to the floor. "I hadn't factored in drying time. This room is going to take longer than expected. At this rate, for the three rooms to be cleaned, primed and painted, the process will use all three free weekends. I have so much more than three weekends worth for you to do. I can't keep you around any longer than stipulated by the charity, unless I start paying you to help me with the bathroom, deck, and kitchen. That's a bundle of money I can't afford yet."

Geoff noticed she was dismayed but only for a few passing moments. To his amazement, the look of defeat turned into one of determination.

"We'll have to work quickly." Her words came fast and clipped. "Prime all three rooms today and hopefully begin with the color for my bedroom tomorrow."

His broad shoulders slumped. He was tired. Working all week with his company and then having to deal with charity work wasn't conducive to relaxation. And, this woman wanted to put hours upon hours of work into one weekend.

"I don't know if it's possible, Tori."

Without responding, she turned her back on him. She rubbed her hands against her jeans, then patted a few fly-a-way strands of hair back into place. Her arms fell to her sides, and she flexed and relaxed her fingers. A few more silent moments passed before she clasped her hands behind her and turned to face him again.

Surprised at her transformation, he gazed at the woman who stood in parade rest, her feet shoulder width apart and her hands behind her back, with her chin jutted out. Her blue-eyed stare, cool and calculating, fixed on his.

He had seen looks like this before but only in important business deals, and the power look suited her. His gaze raked boldly over her. Strong women were such a sexual stimulation for him. His pulse picked up a notch.

"I've had time to consider the situation, Mr. McKenzie," she said matter-of-factly. "It is and will be possible to get this job done. Our systems can handle the work load. We just have to create a program that will fit the needs of the task at hand, install it into our routine and run with it."

He blinked. She didn't move. Not a muscle or eyelid twitched. What happened to the soft, yielding woman he had kissed a few days ago?

"I don't know about your *system*, but mine runs six to seven days a week, twelve to sixteen hours a day. If I keep going, I'll crash."

"You would not crash. We'll have appropriate times to shut down."

What an interesting way of putting things, he thought. And to top it all off, he was aroused. Her paint-splattered, ponytailed hair and her tight-fitting, white-splotched jeans and black t-shirt made her look cute. But the set determination of her face and stance, along with the way she spoke made him imagine her as a dominatrix.

"I won't take no for an answer," she added.

He liked gutsy women. How could he say no to her?

Hell, how could he not say no? He had to. Charity work or not, his well-being and his own business had to come first. He couldn't allow himself to be run into the ground on his own time.

His mouth formed the word he wanted to say, but no sound came out. Damn it all, if he couldn't say it, he would show it.

Carefully, he placed his paint brush in a pan and stood within inches of her. He grabbed the back of her head and brought her face toward his, waiting for her gaze to drop to his lips like they had the other day. Once her gaze lowered, he made his move. His demanding lips caressed hers. She was stiff and unresponsive. He continued the assault until she yielded under his grip and kissed him back. He molded his free hand over her breast and kneaded it. The moment a shuddering sigh escaped from her into his mouth, he stopped, pushed her to arm's length, let her go and walked out.

* * * *

Stunned, Tori stared at his retreating form. He had walked out on her, had left in the middle of a job. He had kissed her again. He had more than kissed her. He'd left her wanting.

How dare he!

She heard a door slam and a vehicle start. She raced to her office window in time to watch the beeping truck back out of the drive.

In her haste to go chase after him, she spun from the window and kicked the frame of the futon. Pain shot up her toes and vibrated through her shin. In a split second, she landed square on her ass on the hard floor.

Frustrated with the turn of events, along with her sexual dissatisfaction, she groaned at her lost opportunity to bring him back. At another stab of pain, she fell back with an irritated sigh. What was with her lately? First she couldn't speak to him. Then she couldn't stop. Then she pulls business jargon on him. It wouldn't surprise her one bit if, after a call from Geoff informing them she was delusional and possessed of multiple personalities, orderlies from the funny farm came and took her away.

There must be a full moon, she rationalized. She rose from the floor and gingerly put weight on her foot.

Gently, she moved and positioned herself to look out the window. She couldn't see the moon. Daylight still reigned outside. But for all she cared, it could have been nighttime. Geoff had gone, and it was as if he had taken the sun with him.

Worse, he had left her with a load of work.

CHAPTER EIGHT

A warm breeze ruffled the curtains of the open windows. The fragrance of late season flowers and the overpowering scent of freshly painted walls stirred Victoria in her sleep. Waking from a dream about a picnic with David under a bright, warm sun, she rolled over and landed on the floor. The combination of the morning sunlight and the white walls of the living room blinded her eyes and her aching muscles screamed.

From her position on the floor, she sat up, stretched and winced from the pain in her arms and legs. She gathered her strength, ignoring her body's protests, and stood. A searing pain shot up her leg. She tumbled back onto the couch.

Furious, she massaged her injured foot, cursing her idiocy which had led her to her present debilitated state. Her foot pounded because she had kicked the futon bed frame. Her body ached because she had gone ahead and continued painting.

Tori bent forward and peered into her office. All the furniture sat in the middle of the floor. A spasm of pain gripped her lower back. She shouldn't have moved the furniture by herself. She shouldn't have gone on to prime the office and the living room afterwards.

Geoff should have stayed to help.

Thinking of the previous afternoon, she ran her fingers through her knotted hair. The proposal she had put to Geoff wasn't out of sorts. It was the same way she bartered when she talked about computer systems. *Computers.* She smacked her forehead. How could she have been so dumb and insensitive? He wasn't one of the networks she worked on, but a human being. He was right. A human body could only handle so much. Her own sore body was a testament to that.

Tori groaned at the thought of all the work that still had to be done, but she couldn't and wouldn't stop now. She always saw her projects through to their end. But how could she finish this project on her own? Another day of hard labor, she'd be flat on her back writhing in agony. Suffering pain due to her stupidity wouldn't do.

She had to swallow her pride and call Geoff again. After all, it was her fault he had left in the first place.

Moments into her cautious, uncomfortable trek toward the office, three fast and loud knocks sounded at her door.

Seems like I won't have to call him. She turned in the direction of the sound.

The banging continued.

"All right, I'm coming," she shouted, limping over to the door. Ready to give Geoff an apology along with a reprimand about being so impatient, she swung it open.

"Hello, Victoria."

Her gaze widened in surprise. She took a deep breath. *Be nice to him. Be polite.* "What do you want, David?" The discomfort of her body brought a heated level of irritation to her voice. She winced at the terseness. *So much for being polite.*

"A good morning to you, too. May I come in?" He took a step forward.

"No." She leaned against the doorway and put her arm out to the side as much as to balance herself as to block his path. "I would prefer if you didn't."

"Why? Do you have...?" David asked, peeking over her shoulder. "My God, your walls!"

Resisting the temptation to look at them, she kept her focus on the man in front of her. "Yes. Quite a difference, isn't it? But if you'll excuse me, I need—"

"I came here to talk." His pale brown eyes implored her as did his voice.

"Well, talk and do it quick. I'm expecting my painter to arrive any moment now, and I'd like to look presentable before he comes."

Seeing David reminded her she hadn't seriously thought about their relationship, and the look of disappointment on his face almost made her sorry for the way she snapped at him. She wished she did have a painter coming. David would leave, and she'd have time to gather her thoughts about him. In fact, the walls could wait another week. She'd gladly give her body a rest and take the time to logically ponder the downward direction of their relationship.

"Painter? I assume that means..."

The sound of a vehicle pulling in front of her house drew David's attention away. Tori's gaze followed his to the red truck parking in her drive.

"You see, he's here, and I'm a mess."

"Well, isn't this interesting." David sneered. He narrowed his stare at the man walking toward them. His back became ramrod straight, then he threw her a heated glare. "We'll talk later, Victoria." With that demand, he turned on his heel and walked away. His squat, square body became pronounced as he neared Geoff's tall, buff physique. David bumped him and kept going.

Apparently startled by the slight, Geoff stopped, looked back at David's retreating form, then to Victoria.

He came back. An electrifying quiver coursed through her body overriding all the pain. *Forget thinking about David.* She took a deep shaky breath, turned and went into the house.

"Don't start getting all flustered," she said to herself, giddy with excitement. She hurried as best she could to the bathroom.

Geoff found her in the small space brushing her hair.

"What was that all about?"

Pulling her tresses up into a ponytail, Tori became self-conscious about him witnessing her in the same clothes as

౷ঔৢঔৢঔৢ

yesterday. Nonetheless, she shrugged off the state of her dress. Clothes should be the least of her worries right now.

"Nothing. He stopped by to talk, but didn't get a chance to." She opened the medicine cabinet and pulled out a bottle. After flipping off the cover, she shook three tablets into her hand then dry-swallowed them.

"Are you all right?"

"Yeah, I'm fine." She turned toward Geoff. His tall, beautifully proportioned body filled the doorway. "You're not going to leave again just because he was here, are you?"

He shook his head.

With his clear and observant gaze on her, the recollection of the kisses and caresses they had shared came to mind. Her body shivered. The bathroom had become too small for her comfort. She fought back the memories and shooed him away from the door.

"Do you want some coffee?" she asked, hoping the chore would be a distraction from him and the raging hormones pinging around in her body.

"Yes. Please."

Out of the corner of her eye, she saw him pull a chair away from the kitchen table, spin it and straddle it. As she prepared a brew strong enough for a caffeine addict, she sensed his gaze on her. Why had he come back? Did he plan to berate her for the way she had acted yesterday? She knew she deserved his rebuke, but still, she couldn't stand reprimands. To prolong the inevitable conversation, she waited till the coffee was done and she had poured a couple of mugs before she turned around.

Geoff's soulful, brown gaze caught and held hers. His kind-hearted expression caused her heart to leap into her throat.

"Tori? About what happened—"

"I meant to call you and apologize about my behavior. My attitude was uncalled for." She placed the mugs on the table and sat down next to him. "I shouldn't have treated the situation like I did."

"Situation? Well, that's one way of looking at it."

"What other way is there? I'll admit how I acted was wrong—"

"Yes, it was."

"If you would just let me finish, I might be able to retain some dignity while I say I'm sorry."

"You're sorry?"

"Why, yes, it is possible for me to admit I can be wrong at times and that yesterday it was wrong of me to treat you as I would a client with a computer problem. I shouldn't have expected so much. You're only human."

Behind the mug he held up to his mouth, he laughed.

"What's so funny?"

"Nothing really." He put the mug down. "I do accept your apology. I'm sorry I left the way I did. Blame it on being tired and cranky. It's just that right now we seem to be talking about two different things."

"Two different things?" Baffled, she tilted her head and crinkled her brow.

"Yeah, I was going to apologize for my behavior at that man's house and yesterday before you interrupted me. You see, you're right. I am only human. The liberties I took by kissing you both times were a mistake and for that I am truly sorry."

"It happens." Feeling foolish, she released her clenched fingers from the coffee mug. He regretted his advances toward her and here she was wishing for a repeat performance. "No apologies needed. We'll chalk it up to just one of those things." She took a sip of coffee. "Since we're clearing the air, let's just say we should act more accordingly from now on—employer, employee, friends at most."

"Good. I was thinking the same thing. You're involved already. I'm involved with my business. It's best we forget both incidents happened." He downed the hot, black liquid. "Well, friend, let's get to work."

Time passed silently as they painted. Geoff had suggested they start in her bedroom, one on either side of the doorway and work around the walls till they encountered each other. She had agreed with his plan. The arrangement would save them from painting too close to one another, getting in each other's way and having to keep up a conversation. They needed to concentrate on the work at hand. She needed the time to think.

As she dipped the roller in the paint pan and watched the tiny air bubbles rise and pop open, a heaviness centered in her chest. He had called her friend. There were worse things to be called and she should be happy, be breathing a sigh of relief, not feeling disappointment.

She was involved. She should have been leaping with joy that there would be no more overtures of flirtation or intimacy from Geoff, especially since her relationship with David was so fragile. At this stage she knew another man's advances would only lead to trouble. So, knowing all this, why wasn't her logical mind determining a way to stop the dismay stabbing at her heart?

Tori stopped in mid-stroke and turned to watch Geoff paint in the opposite corner. The outlines of his muscular shoulders strained against the fabric of his t-shirt as he swiped the roller up and down the wall. His dark hair was a deep contrast against the gray-white background.

A silent sigh escaped her lips and she went back to her task. He'd make a great friend. Someone she'd be able to laugh with, have fun around, be able to talk to without feeling like everything she said was analyzed. Yet, she couldn't help but wonder what being his girlfriend would be like, to have the intimacy along with the friendship. Having him on her arm, she'd be the envy of other women. Having him in bed, she'd be...well...like the fun girl she used to be before David.

Not that she had been overly sexually promiscuous, but she knew a thing or two.

In high school, she had gone steady with one boy for two years until they had both gone their separate ways for college. He had only made it to second base with her. During college, she had set her mind on her studies, not on the goal of finding a husband as most of the other girls. She had kept herself out of the dating pool for a long while successfully. Beside, college had been after her brother's incident, and she couldn't have borne to love and lose again so quickly.

Then she had met Jack in her senior year in an elective course. They had sat next to each other, listening to the professor drone on about beasts and beauties, and gods and goddesses. Gradually they had gotten to know each other.

He, too, had been working toward a degree in computers and they had had a lot in common. She had truly believed she had found her soul mate in Jack and he had been her first. After graduation, they had continued dating and had made plans for the future. She had been one of the lucky ones to find a position in her field right out of school. Jack hadn't. They had to wait on their plans for marriage. A year later, he had been offered a job in Europe and had begged her to marry and go with him. She had told him she couldn't leave. Not only did she have a job she loved, her grandmother had been ill. She couldn't leave her family behind. Their relationship had ended.

For a few years, she went out with friends to all kinds of places. It didn't matter if it was a weeknight or weekend, she was where the action was. One party after another, one bar after another, helped to make the time pass. She had a number of one night stands. She had been on a path of self-destruction. That's when she met dirt-bag Steve. God, that had been a horrid year with an even more horrible ending. Then she had met David. He had seemed so calm, so steady. She had felt wanted and needed, and not in a sexual aspect.

৯৯৯৯৯৯

Before she knew what had happened, she had been led into a steady, platonic relationship.

If she had only known then...

"Tori?"

She jumped at Geoff's touch on her shoulder. Paint from her brush splattered everywhere creating white round dots on Geoff, her and the bedroom floor.

"For the past five minutes you've been painting the same spot." Geoff spoke in a gentle tone. "You need a break. Go get cleaned up. I'll finish in here."

"No, I'll stay," she said, shaking her head clear of thoughts. "I'm okay now."

His brown-eyed gaze narrowed and he shrugged his shoulders.

"What time is it anyway?"

He glanced at his watch. "Three-thirty."

"Oh, maybe I will stop for a bit." She laid her roller on the pan.

"I have an idea," he said, wiping his forehead with his forearm. "Let's go out to eat. We've done enough this weekend, you especially, and we both could use a break. Anyway, it's Sunday. We should be relaxing, not working our asses off."

She responded with a dazzling smile.

Behind her the phone rang.

"You should answer that."

"Uh, yeah, you're right. I should, shouldn't I?"

Tori turned on her heel and hurried to the phone. A few kind words, a suggestion from Geoff and she turned to mush. She must have looked like a bumbling idiot. Dinner out with him wasn't going to be a date, just two friends eating together. *But the way he kept saying we...*

She picked up the portable phone out of its cradle. "Hello?"

Silence hung heavy on the other end.

࿐ᔥ࿐ᔥ࿐ᔥ

"Hello?" She drew out the question.

Faint breathing sounded on the other end of the line.

"Who is this?" Alarm sounded in her voice.

"Victoria? Is everything all right?" Geoff's voice boomed close by.

She heard a low growl, then a click.

She stared at the phone in her hand, then placed it back in the charger. When she entered the bedroom, Geoff stood there, his forehead knotted in concern.

"What was that about?"

"I don't know." She sat on the bed, the protective cover crinkled under her butt. "It must have been a prank. No one spoke. Just silence and some breathing."

"Weird."

She nodded, trying to shake off a chill slithering up and down her spine.

"Well," Geoff said with a slap of the brush to the wall. "Let's finish this last bit, then we'll part, clean up and regroup for dinner."

"Sounds good to me," she mumbled, still perplexed. The call was weird all right. Her number was unlisted, unpublished, un-everything.

CHAPTER NINE

*A*ll was silent and dark, save for the tapping of fingers on the keyboard, the glow of the computer screen and one small desk lamp. Even though it was the middle of the night, conversations between on-line chatters raged at full speed.

LEIME: CX u r up pretty L8—or early—for your neck of the woods. Whatcha doin?
CHAOS_X: Working. Forget where I live. Shouldn't have told.

It had been an hour since initial log-on and already two of the rules Chaos_X and Chaos_Z had set were broken. One, never give out personal information no matter how vague, and two, be on time. Rule one had gone out the window due to boredom and because LEIME, from the exotic land of Hawaii, with its beautiful beaches, warm climate and volcanoes, had sounded interesting. Now the chatter was a nuisance.

LEIME: Working at this hour? Forget? Not like East coast gives exact address. How about having some fun?
CHAOS_X: Not interested.
LEIME: No? What? u have hot date there?
CHAOS_X: I'm waiting for someone. Find someone in Hawaii to talk to.
CHAOS_X: WHERE THE HELL ARE YOU Z?

Immediately three different chatters rolled onto the screen telling CHAOS_X not to scream.

LEIME: I can take a hint. Good bye!
CHAOS_Z: Don't scream again. I'm here.
CHAOS_X: About time. You're late. Private. Now.

Within seconds, CHAOS_X created and opened a private room only accessible to the two of them.

CHAOS_X: Where have you been? Time is of the essence.
CHAOS_Z: Sorry. Was out. Fell asleep. Just woke up. Have news for you.
CHAOS_X: Do tell.
CHAOS_Z: Target sighting confirmed. Source reliable.
CHAOS_X: Really? Go on.
CHAOS_Z: Busy at house...long time. Went out to dinner. Becoming close if know what mean.
CHAOS_X: I catch your drift.
CHAOS_Z: Source says, most time in bedroom... dinner intimate.
Seconds passed. CHAOS_X breathed hard trying to control an uprising of anger.
CHAOS_Z: U there?
CHAOS_X: Yes. Just thinking. I feel like chess.
CHAOS_Z: ???
CHAOS_X: Never mind. Anything else?
CHAOS_Z: Not at the moment. So what's the deal?
CHAOS_X: Don't know. It's too late or too early to come up with anything good right now. But I will. Don't worry, I'll think better after I get some sleep.
CHAOS_Z: Chat same time same place tomorrow night?
CHAOS_X: Yes. And be on time.
CHAOS_Z: Sure thing.

The chatters logged off. CHAOS_X pulled a leather bound journal from its hiding spot, opened the book and put pen to paper to vent before the see red rage became too consuming.

CHAPTER TEN

"*H*ey, cuz, where ya been?" Philip leaned against the open refrigerator door, holding a slice of bread with layers of ham in one hand and a bottle of mustard in the other.

Geoff's eyes, along with all his muscles from the strain of the past several days, ached with fatigue. He was so tired he couldn't even reprimand his cousin for making a sandwich straight off the shelves.

"I've been out," he grunted and watched Philip poise the mustard high above the meat and bread. His cousin gave the bottle a good squeeze. The thick yellow substance squirted out too fast, splattering the pink layers of meat and the black and white tiled floor. Yellow dots littered the checkered pattern at his feet.

The steak and shrimp platter, complete with salad, vegetables and potato as well as the side order of wings Geoff ate during his dinner with Victoria churned in his gut. The last thing he needed was to look at more food or his cousin. A low growl escaped his throat.

"Don't worry," Philip spoke with a full mouth. "I'll clean up."

Geoff didn't think his cousin sounded contrite, but nodded his head anyway, then made his way into the brightly lit living room. He fell onto the black leather couch back first and was blinded by the glare of the recessed lighting. He'd have to put in a dimmer switch if Philip continued to keep the living room fully illuminated. Either that or get some shaded table lamps and disconnect the ceiling lights. Maybe then he would feel like he was at home instead of at the office.

Tracked

ৰ‌ঌ‌ৰ‌ঌ‌ৰ‌ঌ

Home. What an elusive word. To his way of thinking, it went hand in hand with happiness. And both had evaded him most of his life. Yet, if the old adage *home is where you hang your hat* was true, then he'd have to say this was his home.

Everything he had put in the house and done to the property reflected who he had become. The black leather couch, recliner and love seat beckoned one to feel their softness, note their expense. Aligned meticulously with the furniture were the glass coffee and end tables. Suppressing a chuckle, Geoff recalled the astonished look on the salesman's face when he had requested the green-tinted, clouded glass originally put with the sterling silver frames to be replaced with non-tinted, crystal clear glass. The salesman had balked. Geoff had paid extra, but the expense had been worth it. He wanted to be able to see through the tables to his light gray carpet.

Gray. They had painted Victoria's bedroom a shade of gray. Granted, the hue appeared white, but with closer inspection, one could see there was a nuance of color. His gaze grazed over his walls. Color was what his place lacked. All his walls had been painted with the starkest white he could find. The black and white abstract prints he had hung added no interesting shades, either. He hadn't been striving for a warm, homey feeling, though, when he had decorated. What he had wanted to achieve was a look that said he had made it, he was a success and he could afford the finer things. Now that the look was achieved, he wasn't happy with the effects at all.

Philip's heavy footed steps approached. He opened his eyes.

"Well?" Philip threw himself haphazardly into the recliner, yet not dropping a crumb of food from the sandwich he had yet to finish.

"I'm thinking about redecorating."

ৰ‌ঌ‌ৰ‌ঌ‌ৰ‌ঌ

"Redecorating? Thought you liked your black and whites. You know, black, white, nothing in between, nothing hidden, no having to explain…"

"Enough, Phil."

"Sorry man." Philip picked up the bottle of beer he had left on the coffee table and took a swig. "Well?"

"Well, what?" Geoff didn't try to hide his annoyance or his glare at the filmy ring left behind on the glass. Phil knew he needed to use coasters.

"Where ya been out to?" Phil asked eagerly.

"I went out to dinner." He thought for a moment about Victoria and her house. Once the place was complete, her home would have a lived-in feeling with its light earth tones and rich color borders. She was the type who wouldn't care about rings on the table and would say the marks lent to the lived-in feeling and could be cleaned up. Her coasters most likely would be out in plain sight and ready for use anyway, not hidden away in a drawer in the kitchen. He shook his head. How two houses and two lives only miles apart could actually be two different worlds amazed him.

"I'm surprised you're home, Phil, and not out with your love *d'jour*, miss high and mighty, Stephanie."

"*Shvetng amlee.*"

"Don't talk with your mouth full." *Why did he let his cousin live with him?* "Didn't Aunt Cheryl teach you any manners?"

Philip's throat bulged. "Sure. Mom taught me plenty. Like I said, Steph's visiting family. I didn't want to be bored all weekend, so I stayed back."

"Lucky me," he quipped, but understood why Phil had stayed back. Stephanie and her old moneyed family enjoyed looking down their noses at people, especially those who had worked hard and created their own wealth. Normally, people like that didn't bother his carefree, *who cares what people think* cousin. He could handle them one on one with his witty, sarcastic charm. Stick him in a room full of the ultra-snobs, though, and he was out of his league.

How Philip and Steph had hooked up was still a mystery to him. Sure, Phil only seemed to date beautiful women and Stephanie fit the bill, but what she saw in laid-back, unpretentious Philip, he didn't know.

What he did believe was that Phil and Steph's relationship wouldn't last much longer. The two of them were not compatible together. But he wasn't going to tell Phil his thoughts on the matter. He closed his eyes again.

"Looks like you were put through the ringer." Phil laughed. "Is Bertha Sims up to her old tricks again?"

"Kind of. Did I mention she and her mother were at the auction?"

"Yeah, and lucky for you they didn't get the bid. Who was it that hired you? Sally... Sally...?"

"Becker. She's part owner of CompNet Incorporated."

"Omp et?" Phil chewed over the word. There was a pause. "CompNet? I called that company today."

"You did what?" Geoff bolted upright.

"Hey, don't get peeved, man. You told me to find a new IT service several weeks ago. You said we needed a better computer system since we're growing so fast. I finally took the initiative. The customer service representative said they'd put the order through and send out a field rep. Someone by the name of Victoria...Victoria Patton."

"It's Padden...d, d, e...and you'll have to call them back. Request someone else."

"Someone else?" Philip's jade-eyed gaze widened at the order. "Why? With a name like Victoria she's bound to be pretty and I might—"

"You might not do anything except call and request someone different." *She's beautiful.* The uncensored thought and protective urge that swelled up in Geoff jarred his senses.

He took a deep breath, then murmured, "It would be a conflict of interest otherwise."

"Mmmm hmmm, looks like Geoff's found himself a girlfriend. You didn't tell me you were dating again."

"I'm not dating again. She's Sally's employee and Sally subcontracted me out to her to finish off the time from the charity. We're business associates. That's all." Was it? The memory of how eager he was to see her again after only a few short hours, along with her image, sprang to his mind. The dark blue denim dress she had worn on their *date* had dramatized her big blue eyes. Tori had also worn her hair down and the locks had rested upon her shoulders in soft golden brown waves.

He realized he wasn't attracted to just her looks anymore, either. As she had answered his questions all evening, he had found her to be beautiful inside as well as out. She had seemed eager for his attention and hadn't minded telling him about herself. Though, at first, she had been the demure female saying she didn't want to bore him. But after he had insisted, mentioning that if they were to be friends they'd have to talk about themselves, he couldn't get her to stop. She was like a dam that had burst open and all her information was full of animation. Tori had chatted away about her job duties and promotion and how she had excelled in school.

The one thing he observed that had quieted her were the wide-eyed, curious stares of a young woman sitting at a table with another female in the bar section. Periodically, throughout their meal, she had kept glancing over at the pair, catching the younger female watching them. He had no clue who the lady or her companion was and neither did she. The companion had worn a pair of sunglasses and had a scarf draped over her head, hiding her hair. She had never turned around to look at whom the young lady obviously spoke about.

The whole situation had made Tori antsy. He had barely heard her mumble something about the phone call, but couldn't mistake her growing anxiety when she had made an overly loud remark about how rude some people were.

He had tried to lighten the mood by complimenting her, remarking on the woman's jealousy of Tori's beauty. The words had gone unnoticed. Instead, she had shaken her head, murmuring about happenstance.

Was there a connection between the phone call she had received and the people at the restaurant? No. There couldn't be. As Tori had said, it was only a coincidence.

And when it came to chance occurrences, it was a good thing she had come around and talked about David. They had met a couple of years ago when she had begun working on the Valley View Clinic's computer system. Since he practiced there, once they had started dating she had to transfer the account to another representative.

He had been surprised how much her speaking about her ex-boyfriend bothered him, but he found the more she went on, the more he wanted to know about her, the good and the bad. Though he inwardly cringed every time that man's name rolled over her lips, he was now thankful. Otherwise he wouldn't have known her working on his company's computer system would be a problem.

"Mmm hmm. Yeah, that's all. Mmm hmm. Only friends," Philip sang into Geoff's thoughts, taunting him. "Connflieeect of Innnteressst. Mmm hmm. Sure. Ooh, yeah. I gotta me a woomaan. Fine as she can beee. Her name is Victoria. She's the one for meee."

"Will you cut out that racket?" Geoff put his hands up to his ears.

"Mmm hmm. Ooh, yeah. There. I'm done."

"Thank you." Geoff lay back down on the couch. He didn't really hate Philip's singing. Out of all the McKenzie and Sterling blood relations, he ran a close second to Sean who had the best voice. All the men could sing, except for Alec. The poor guy couldn't carry a tune to save his life, but he was a great shot with a camera. Remembering how Sean and Philip used to enter contests and bring girls to their knees with their voices, Geoff smiled. Their competing had gotten to the point where they had won so many awards the two of them had considered forming their own band, Sterling McKenzie. Sean and Philip would sing, he would manage, and Alec would do the public relations and covers. The group of them had had big plans once. Only Sean pursued a singing career now. Funny how life changed along the way.

"So tell me about her. I'd like to know who my cousin is pining for."

"I won't get any peace if I don't, will I?" Geoff asked through gritted teeth, hating having his thoughts interrupted constantly, and sat back up.

"That's right, my good man." Phil chuckled. "It's been a long time since you've dipped into the feminine pool. I'm hoping this time you've met someone, um, normal."

"Victoria's normal. She's a lovely lady," Geoff said with a sigh. "Intelligent, talented. From what I gather her family seems to be well off. Her father is vice president of a real estate franchise and knows how to invest. Her mother stays home. They live in upstate New York. She lives across the river in Hillsborough in what used to be her grandparents' house. As for her shoe size, I don't know."

"Hmm... Did she learn anything about you or did you play the mysterious McKenzie as usual?"

"I let her talk."

"No wonder women leave you."

He shot his cousin a *don't you go there* look.

"Hey, cuz, I'm just trying to help. If you don't let them into your world, how are you going to carry on any kind of relationship?" Philip didn't get an answer. "Are you going to see her again?"

"Yeah, next weekend. I have to continue my charity work at her place."

"You gonna ask her out?"

"Like I said, we're business associates. We're working together. Besides, I don't think her boyfriend would like it too much if I asked her out." Okay, so she wasn't really attached anymore and David was an ex, but he tired of his cousin's prying. "Now, if we're finished, I'm going to bed."

As Geoff walked up the stairs, Philip sang one last time, "Boyfriend. Dum da dum dum. Ooh, yeah."

Geoff stretched out on his bed and lay awake in the darkness. His cousin was right. He wouldn't get anywhere in a relationship if he didn't reciprocate. He should have told her about himself. After all, friendships couldn't be one-sided.

He would have to open up and convey his memories of his truck driving father who was never around, but didn't seem to mind moving his family from state to state. He would have to relate the experience of seeing his mother grow old before her time because she had to raise her three children on her own.

How would Tori react? He didn't grow up wealthy. She was used to money, if having a rich friend like Sally, having dated a doctor and attending charity events were any indication. Would she mind he had created his own business? That his endeavor had only started to turn a profit a few years ago? And would she care he and Phil barely had their heads out of the water? He wished he didn't have to tell her anything. Opening himself up to her would only hurt more in the end when she left him. But their relationship was based on friendship and friends stuck by each other, didn't they?

The thought brought little comfort.

He rolled over and punched his pillow. From his viewpoint, his other girlfriends, and his wife, had no reasons to turn their backs on him either. But they had. One of these days, he'd love to find out why.

CHAPTER ELEVEN

*E*xhaustion overwhelmed Tori as she followed a client out of the building. The past two days had been hectic. Unfortunately, it wasn't for her own purposes. The people of one of her contracts called late Friday afternoon stating they needed to be up and running by Monday. Forced to sacrifice her personal time, and that of her interns, they spent the weekend at Greentree office running cables and setting up servers. Her back ached from lugging around heavy boxes, bundles of wires and from sleeping on a rickety cot. Her head pounded from her interns' constant bickering and concern if Geoff had been able to get any work done at her house. She'd hidden a note and a key for him, chilled some beers in the fridge, then left him a message about it all, but she never heard back.

Even with all the personal turmoil going on, the team had accomplished enough to satisfy the client. Granted, she had allowed a couple of nonessential programs to go uninstalled. But according to the company manual and the fact that during the first few days she'd be there while the employees were training, she didn't see the lack of complete installs to be a problem. She'd finish installing the extraneous programs when she returned in the morning.

With her mind on those thoughts and the need for quiet solitude, she drove the few minutes home on autopilot. On her way in, she grabbed her mail out of the mailbox.

Balancing her purse, overnight bag and mail on one side of her body, she fumbled in the dim overhead light with her key to unlock the door. As it swung open, she flipped on the lights and took in a startled breath. Gone was the green. The walls were a soothing color of beige. Geoff had come and had finished painting her living room.

With a small exclamation of glee, she threw the mail onto the coffee table, dropped her bags, and rushed into her office. All the furniture was back in place. Off-white walls claimed the boundaries of the room. The space finally looked like a true office. Her own home office. An air of triumph expanded her chest.

Tori ran into her bedroom, and the sight took her breath away. The room was beautiful. She was pleasantly surprised he had taken the time to hang the border, the royal blue curtains and valance. She took a few steps. The lack of sound brought her attention to her feet. A large, thick material area rug covered a good portion of the floor. Bold black and white lines outlined the gray rectangular center in the middle of it. Kneeling down, she lifted a corner and noticed a thin layer of padding under it. When she rose, a single long stemmed white rose on her new burgundy comforter caught her eye. Next to it was a note and her key. She flung herself on the bed, grabbed the paper and read it aloud.

"Sorry I missed you, Victoria. I hope everything is to your satisfaction. We'll finish up the final details later. Don't worry about the rug. I remembered I had it stowed away in my attic. I have no use for it so it's yours. I hope your weekend went well. Thanks for the beer. G."

With the letter in hand, she sprang from the bed and trotted to the bathroom. The washroom looked different and larger somehow. The gaudy floral wallpaper was gone, replaced with the plain light beige.

Yes, she was very satisfied. She placed the paper against her chest with her hands crossed over it and a sense of completion filled her soul. She'd have to find a way to show Geoff her appreciation.

Divining a plan, amongst other things, would have to wait, though. Since she hadn't had time during the week, a pile of mail needed her attention first. Then there was the bath she had promised herself.

From her office she retrieved the parcels, and in the living room, added the new pieces of correspondence to the pile on coffee table. Within minutes, she had all the mail sorted into three stacks—bills, junk to read and junk to be thrown out— and one straggler—a plain white envelope.

Her heart raced lightly, wondering who would leave a plain white envelope in her mailbox. Curious to see what the person had to say, she tore open the lone piece of mail. She pulled out a heavy piece of typing paper and unfolded it.

One boldly typed phrase was in the center.

CEASE AND DESIST.

A lump formed in her throat. She stared down at the paper trembling in her hands. *What the hell did that mean? Cease and desist. And who the hell put this in my mailbox?*

Maybe it was Geoff's way of saying the work was finished. She shook her head. No, it wasn't finished and somehow she knew he wouldn't have put that it was in such a manner or typed it.

Perhaps a neighbor? Someone who didn't like her fixing up the place? She did have some neighbors neither she nor her grandparents had gotten along with and others who were nosy and looking for something to complain about. She shook her head again. They may complain, but they were barkers, not biters, surely not the kind to act on their complaints.

Could someone be warning her she needed a permit? She didn't think she needed one, not for painting, but to be sure she jotted down a note to call the municipal building in the morning.

She crumpled the note in her hand. Why couldn't whoever had written it just have said what they meant and not have been so vague?

David.

His name rattled around in her mind for a few moments. What if the short note *had* been from David? She wouldn't put it past him, especially with how he had been acting lately and her lack of contact. He hadn't been too pleased with her and his dislike of Geoff was apparent. Could he be jealous? She chuckled. There was nothing to be jealous about because she and Geoff were only friends. It was still a possibility, though, and she figured the only way to find out would be to call him. Tired as she was, she knew all too well she wouldn't be able to sleep until her mind was put to rest about this.

Tori reached for her phone. It rang the moment she touched it. No number showed on the caller identification, but she didn't find that out of the ordinary. Taking the call, she hoped it was nothing to do with a client's system—though it probably was—since she really needed a few hours to herself and a good night's sleep. "Hello?"

"He's mine, you know," an angry voice shouted. The words sounded muffled, metallic.

"Excuse me?"

"He's mine. You best be remembering it."

"Who is this?" Alarm bells went off in her, sending ringing vibrations of cold through her system. She choked back rising fear and anger.

"Does it matter who this is? I'm tired of being put on the back burner. I'm tired of not being recognized. I'll have no one getting in my way."

Tori frantically searched her mind to match the caller to someone she knew only to realize the voice was too distorted. The person had to be talking through a device attached to the handset. Plus, with all the people she came in contact with, there were too many voices, too many faces to even start to compare.

Who would do this to her? If it was just a prank, it was a really sick joke. Playing on somebody's fears, on something that happened in the past. Not nice. Not nice at all. "Who are you? How did you get my number?"

"You of all people should realize information, no matter how private, is obtainable with a few clicks of a keyboard."

The blood rushed from her face and limbs, leaving in its wake frigid swaths of skin as the words and the sound of a disconnected line sank in.

It was true. People could find out anything they wanted if they knew how. Even she had been known once in a while to track people down who hadn't wanted to be found.

With a shaking finger, she hit the off button of her cordless, then went to the charging cradle and unplugged the phone.

CHAPTER TWELVE

CHAOS_Z: I've gotten the ball rolling and have more ideas.
CHAOS_X: That's great. I, too, have a plan.
CHAOS_Z: Care to share?

For the next fifteen minutes the two chatters bantered back and forth in their private room exchanging their thoughts, elaborating on some, dispelling others. By the time they finished, a stratagem was in place along with alternatives they both were pleased with and agreed upon.

CHAOS_Z: Some of this sounds a little dangerous to me. We aren't going to get caught are we?
CHAOS_X: I should think not. Then again, how do I know we can trust your source not to spill the beans?
CHAOS_Z: My source is trustworthy. No beans will be spilt.
CHAOS_X: I should hope not. Besides, our plans probably won't go that far. I wouldn't worry if I were you.
CHAOS_Z: I'm not. You're right.
CHAOS_X: I'm sure everything will work out just fine.

The chatter pulled out the journal, read through some entries, then found a blank page.

Bastards and bitches, every one of them. Why? Because they can talk to him, enjoy his company, touch him. And that one woman, the biggest bitch of all, in the house with him. God only knows what's going on there.

Nothing I do will ever be enough until I have him for myself.

CHAPTER THIRTEEN

"*A*nd then he said he wanted me to..." The young woman's voice fell to a whisper. A few moments later her companion let out a screech of laughter.

"He didn't."

"He sure did. And me, being the nice gal I am, had to comply. When I got down on my knees, he said real husky like, 'Ah, the things we'll do together.' And I..."

I can't stand to listen to this anymore, Victoria thought and was up in a flash on her feet looking into the cubicle next to hers.

"Ladies, your discussion is to end here and now. Not only is it inappropriate to banter on about your sexual conquests, something which should be a private matter between the two parties involved, it is especially inappropriate here at work. If you feel the need to compare notes, I suggest you do it on your own time, outside of the office environment. I, for one—and I'm sure I speak for any others within hearing distance—don't want to hear about you and your studs any longer."

The girls, stunned into silence, gaped at her. Satisfied with her reprimand, Tori returned to her chair.

"If anyone needs to get laid, it's her."

"You got that right, sister."

Tori shook her head. The young women were right. She did need a good romp in the sack. Her celibacy had lasted too long, and she was ripe for the picking. Having sex would probably clear the cobwebs from her head and relax her better than anything else she could do. She glanced at the phone.

Geoff. Maybe if she played her cards right, he could scratch her itch.

She shook her head again, this time to clear it before any lusty thoughts decided to intrude, and took her mail from her in-box. She was afraid to look at the pile. It was bad enough she didn't like to hear her phone ring since she had received a handful of prank calls each day. Now, her mail didn't hold a special place in her heart. The three envelopes tucked away in her purse had deadened any joy she had ever had for receiving mail, personal or otherwise.

Each day's letter burned and flashed in her memory. Sunday's was CEASE AND DESIST. Monday's read the same as Sunday's, but had NOT YOUR MAN written at the bottom. Tuesday's stated THE GRASS ISN'T GREENER ON THE OTHER SIDE.

Another note or two and more prank calls, and she might go to the police. Her whole body shuddered. She hated the police and dreaded facing any of those men in uniform. All their rules and regulations. She could still hear the officers' voices. *Sorry we can't help you. Not without more proof.* They'd tell her the same thing now if she brought the letters in and explained the phone calls.

As for that time years ago, if it weren't for the other woman...

"Tori?"

She jumped and stared at her phone.

"Tori, are you there?" Sally's boxed voice quizzed through the intercom.

"Yes, I'm here, Sally."

"Good. How was your morning at Greentree?"

"It went very well. All the programs are installed. The reps had some hands-on training. They're a quick bunch. Didn't take them long at all to learn what they needed."

"That's because they had a good teacher. Did you get their firewalls up?"

"Sid and Keith are working on that."

"Do you think they're advanced enough for that on their own? If they miss anything, Greentree's files will be free for the taking anytime anyone's on the net."

Remembering the prank call Sunday night, Tori cringed. The voice had pointed out how any information could be had for those who knew the ways.

"I'm aware of that, yes." All too well, she added silently. "Internet and Web Publishing were part of their curriculum last year, and from how they talk, they seem to know more than I do. They created programs in their class for some of the science departments at the school. Then they had some hacker buddies of theirs try to break through. Their friends couldn't break in. Sid and Keith's walls were impenetrable. Needless to say, the science departments were very pleased their experiments were safe. And, before you ask, no I didn't take their words for it. I checked out the details for myself at the college."

"Okay, then…" Sally paused. "You do understand if they screw up, it reflects on you."

"Yes, Sally, I know. They won't screw up."

The line went quiet. Tori rifled through her small stack of correspondence. She wasn't surprised to find three memos and two pieces of computer-based junk mail, but she was surprised when a pristine white envelope with her name typed on it lay on her desk. Her hands shook as she tore it open and pulled out the familiar piece of typing paper.

DON'T BE WITH WHOM YOU DON'T BELONG.

Her blood ran cold.

The paper quivered in her trembling fingers. A thousand questions raced through her mind. All the typical journalistic ones… Who? What? Where? When? How? If she were a news reporter, she'd have her bases covered. She restrained a nervous chuckle. Now all she needed to make this complete was one of those prank calls. As if on cue, her phone rang. She jolted at the sound, and with each ring, took in a deep breath to steady her frazzled nerves. She answered on the fifth.

"Victoria Padden. How may I serve you?" As always, she made sure there was a pleasant lilt to her voice with emphasis on the *serve*. It was an inside trade joke most people didn't get, but she thought it added a nice touch.

"My, you sound chipper this morning."

"Hello, David." Her voice went flat.

"Sounds like you were expecting someone else."

"What can I do for you?"

"Could we get together this afternoon? Lunch, perhaps? Say twelve-thirty at Nespo's?"

Tori thought for a long moment, letting his request hang in the air. If Geoff called while she was out of the office, his message would go into her voice mail, so it wasn't as if she would miss his call. On the other hand, she did have a lot of work to do. She sighed. One hour of her time with David couldn't be that bad. Work or no work, she needed to eat and they needed to talk.

"I'm busy today, but I guess I could fit you in for an hour."

"Great. Oh, and we'll go Dutch."

Always the cheap one... "Fine." She hung up the phone.

At the appointed time, she walked into the small restaurant and let her eyes adjust to the dim interior. The few times she and David had been there she'd thought the subdued lighting had added to the romance of the cozy restaurant. Now it annoyed her. All she wanted to do was find David, have each of them say their piece and leave.

She scanned the room and noticed a few men sitting at the bar eating their lunches. David sat toward the back and waved to her. Once she reached his table, he rose and gave her a tiny kiss on each cheek.

"Have a seat. It's great to see you. You look nice. I'm sorry I didn't call sooner. I meant to, but with work and the house… Well, you know how it is."

"Yes, I know." *Yeah, too wrapped up in yourself.* She looked down and fiddled with a rhinestone pin on her lapel.

"I see that's a new suit."

"Yes, it is." She had bought the midnight blue dress the day before in a rare moment of shopping spontaneity. Geoff had been on her mind. She'd thought he might like it. She smiled.

"My God, Victoria, it's great to see you and your smile again. You seem different. There's contentment in your face. I've..."

Interrupted by the waiter, the two of them watched silently as he set down drinks and an order of garlic bread.

"Your food will be out shortly." He bowed his head and left.

"I hope you don't mind," David said, once the waiter took his leave. "I took the liberty and ordered. I figured since you said you were busy you'd want to keep this lunch short and sweet. I got your favorite—linguine with chicken and white sauce and a garden salad."

"Thank you," she replied for lack of anything better to say. David was pleasant and considerate, so unlike his normal self. *He's up to something. There's a reason why I'm here.* Before she could voice a question to her thoughts, David threw her another curve ball.

"My treat."

"What happened to going Dutch?"

"I changed my mind, if that's okay? I know how you like to be independent and make your own way, but I thought it'd be nice to be traditional for once. If you still feel the need to pay..."

"Oh, no, it's fine. Unexpected is all. I do appreciate it and thank you again." She took a bite of bread. "Mmmm, they make a great loaf."

"That they do."

"David, you were saying something when the waiter came over. Does it have to do with why we're here?"

"Ah, my logical, Victoria." David leaned back in the chair, placing his hands in his lap. "Needing a reason for everything. Why A should equal B, and if it does, does it affect C? Perhaps I only wanted to be with you."

She arched an eyebrow.

"Well, okay, yes, there is a more solid reason, though my wanting to be with you should have been more than enough." He sighed. "Like I was saying, I've missed you, Victoria. Terribly. I didn't call because I thought you were angry with me, so I decided to give you some time. After a week passed, I had hoped you would call me. When you didn't, I really knew you were angry. I had stopped over that day to talk and apologize, but you weren't being very receptive. Then that man showed." He paused and closed his eyes for a moment. "I surmised you still needed some space, so I let you have it. Many times I sat by the phone knowing I should pick it up, call you and apologize for my insensitivity, but I was afraid to." He chuckled. "I truly am sorry about our misunderstanding those few weeks ago. I should have been more aware of your feelings. It was a very nice gesture, you bringing in that man to help out on the house. Especially since it was free. But I should have been told of your plans. You know I like to be in some control when it comes to my house."

Sat by the phone? That man? Some control? She put a clamp on her thoughts by biting her tongue and counting to ten. "Yes. Right." She hoped he'd notice she wasn't apologizing. "Total lack of communication."

"Yes, it was." David nodded. "After this weekend passed, I decided I had to be the one to make the move. We haven't seen each other in so long. It's my fault. Lately I've been somewhat of a bear to be around."

Tori snorted. "You can say that again."

"Perhaps it would have been better if we had waited a little while longer before we had moved in together. But, we can't change what we did."

"David, moving in together had and has nothing to do with your attitude. You've been a bear for the past year and have progressively gotten worse. I've been trying to give you a chance because we were happy with each other five months ago. We seemed to like being with each other then and through the previous year."

"That's true."

Silence passed between them for several minutes before she spoke again. "Remember when you started courting me, David? You'd send me flowers and funny little cards at work on a regular basis. They made me smile and made my days better."

"The florist was on my speed dial. It had become so much of a routine, we had devised codes for what was to be sent so I wouldn't have to describe what I wanted each time."

"I didn't know that." She took a sip of wine. "Then there was the time we went to the carnival and acted like two kids. We both ate so much cotton candy and other junk food we ended up with stomach cramps and couldn't make it into work the next day."

"That was the first time you stayed over at my house," he said wistfully. "That night and the following day we had watched so many romantic comedies we laughed till we cried. Didn't help our stomachs, did it?"

"No, and I haven't been able to eat, much less look at cotton candy since."

"How about that time for your birthday when I put you on a riddle quest that led you down to the rental house at the shore?"

"I remember. For a week, I received your hints at work. A message in a bottle, that tongue twister about sea shells, a ceramic horse figurine, a Bon Jovi CD and a treasure map with only lines and numbers. When Friday rolled around, I still hadn't guessed where you wanted me to find you until I showed Sally the clues. She told me I was to meet you at that bar in Seaside and called me stupid for not figuring it out. I had to remind her I grew up in New York. I was so tired when I finally got there and found you. You could have told me traffic to the shore is horrendous on a Friday evening in the summer."

"Sorry about that. It must have slipped my mind."

"Well," she said, smiling with the pleasurable memories and at the hint of humor she had heard in his voice a moment before. "The pearls you gave me made up for it."

"We've had some good times together, haven't we?"

"I guess you can say we had some."

"Tori, I hope I can make up for a lot of things. As you've stated, this past year hasn't been all that great. I'm under the gun trying to get my damn dissertation done. I'm only halfway through, and I only have six months left to complete it. The partners at the clinic are hounding me about it. They want my degree up on the wall so I can take a larger client base. Plus...there have been some other setbacks..."

"David, if you need money, I've—"

"No!" He bolted upright in his chair, took a steadying breath, then leaned back. "No. It's nothing now. I've already figured out a way to handle it."

"Oh, all right then." Contrite, she looked down at the table. "Just thought I'd offer."

"I appreciate your concern but...never mind. Anyway, I'd like to get back what we once had. I'd like to see that smile of yours directed toward me every day."

She watched him reach inside his jacket and pull out a small black box. Her stomach tightened, then rolled with queasiness. David leaned over the table and held the box out to her. Instead of reaching for it as was expected, she put her hands in her lap, tightly entwining her fingers together.

At the same moment David presented the box, the waiter came and put their food in front of them. She hardly noticed his presence since her sight was consumed with the box. Any trace of appetite had disappeared.

Maybe it's a bracelet, a necklace, a pair of earrings. A peace offering.

"Victoria, I'd like you to marry me. I don't want us to be apart ever again. I need you. I need you to be in my life."

"You need me?" She gripped her hands tighter together in her lap. *What about love?* Jack had gone down on one knee cradling a dozen red roses, which hid two plane tickets, and had held out a box with a plain gold band in his free hand. When he had proposed, he had pledged his undying love and loyalty.

"But, of course." His eyebrows drew together in seeming confusion. "I need you to help me take care of things. I've felt lost without you these past weeks." With the box placed snugly in his hand, he flipped the top open with his thumb and forefinger.

She stared at the sparkling princess cut diamond in the white gold band. The jewel was at least a carat. On each side were small square emeralds.

His financial hardship mustn't have been too bad for him to afford such an expensive ring. Unless the jewelry was what he meant.

"It was my grandmother's," he said in line with her thoughts. "I'd be proud if you were to wear it. Please say you'll marry me."

৯৬৫৬৬৫৬৬৫৬

Stunned into silence, she looked up from the ring to David—plump, rounded David with his pug little nose and holier-than-thou attitude. Her mind flashed to Geoff—tall, handsome Geoff who made her laugh. Yet, she and Geoff had decided they were friends, nothing more, and someone out there didn't even seem to like that.

She kept her stare trained on the man in front of her, realizing she hadn't had the time to make a simple phone call to find out if he was the one behind those stupid notes she had been receiving. Though he was in the middle of a proposal, she figured the current moment was as good a time as any to see if he was the culprit.

"Cease and desist."

"Excuse me?"

The man didn't even flinch. If he had any idea of what she had said, she was sure he would have had some kind of reaction. *Oh, well, so much for it being him.*

"David, I don't know what to say."

"Say yes." He flashed what she had always thought to be his fake smile. The one he used for humoring patients.

"I can't." Her gaze flitted from his to the beautiful ring and back. "Several times I tried to talk to you about getting engaged, eventually getting married. Just talk, and you wanted nothing to do with the conversation. What makes you think…" Tori shook her head. "I have to think about this. I can't answer right away." She pushed away from the table and stood. Pulling some money out of her wallet, she added, "This is to cover my untouched food. I wouldn't feel right making you pay for something I didn't eat."

"You don't have to go."

The sadness in his voice made her heart go out to him, but she held back any signs of that showing.

Tori laid the money on the table. "Yes, I do."

She drove around aimlessly for the rest of the afternoon, contemplating her future. Before the sky began to grow dark, she ended up on Sally's porch.

Inside, she explained all the events leading up to her appearance on Sally's doorstep, apologizing the whole time for not returning to work. When she was done, Sally began an unrelenting diatribe.

"I don't know what you've seen in him, anyway." Sally said for the tenth time in as many minutes. "A friend of mine used to be a patient of his, but after a few sessions she switched to another practitioner. She said she didn't like his condescending attitude. I don't know how you could take it. Listen to me. Babbling away like a brook. What are you going to do?"

"I don't know." She gnawed on a ragged fingernail.

"You mustn't marry him." Sally narrowed her gaze at Tori, then out the bay window of the family room. She rubbed her chin. "You know I like to give advice and I understand the times when you haven't followed it, but this time, dear, it's different. You must do as I say. Take it as an order from your friend *and* boss. Do *not* marry David."

Should she give up the prospect for security, a constant companion in her life, the fact that her mother would be ecstatic—*a doctor in the family*—even though the affection wasn't there, all for something that may just be a whim? Or should she take a chance and see if she and Geoff could develop a relationship? Victoria turned away, wearied by the tumult of thoughts racing through her head. "I'll take your advice to heart and strongly consider it, but I'm the one who should make the final verdict. Deep down David is a good man…"

Sally huffed, but she ignored it.

"He really can be when he stops being so self-centered. We had a lot of good times together." Tori paused, remembering the pleasant reminiscing she and David had done during lunch. Aware Sally wasn't satisfied with her answers, she added, "Tell you what I'll do, boss. I'll go home, make out a list of pros and cons, and see which weighs more."

"I hope you'll be able to be impartial when you do it."

"So do I," Tori replied in a broken whisper, wishing she didn't have to make the decision.

The two women sat quietly for a moment until Sally, pointing her finger in the air, sprang from the couch.

"What?" Tori leapt up with her. "What is it?"

"Nothing." Sally's expression was a bit puzzled then, in a blink, she smiled. "Nothing's wrong. Just something I had forgotten about till now. Sit tight. I'll be right back." Sally patted her arm, then hurried from the room.

Tori sat back and sipped the tea Sally's maid had brought in earlier. But the drink had grown cold. On the wall across from her hung a painting she still had yet to figure out. She assumed the picture was what artists considered abstract, with its straight lines, square shapes and bright, bold colors. But what was it? Was it a person's face, square-ish and done larger than life? Or a building with a couple of windows, a door and a crack in the middle? Maybe the artist was a beginner in the craft.

"It's whatever you want it to be."

"Excuse me?" she asked, peeling her attention from the weird piece of art to Sally

"It's new. The painting. It's whatever you want it to be. I like to think it's a man—proud, strong, focused on a goal. Anyway, here." She placed two slips of heavy, shiny paper into Tori's hand. "Those are what I almost forgot about. Two tickets for the Children's Charity Banquet this Friday. Frank and I can't go. I want you to go in our place."

"I can't go to this either. You know I'm not a part of the social crowd. I couldn't possibly."

"Nonsense, you can and you will. The tickets are already paid for. I won't accept no for an answer. There will be others going from our company and some of our clients will be there, too. If it makes you feel better, mix some business in. You could invite Geoff."

That would make for an interesting evening out. She absentmindedly played with the tickets. "Okay. I'll go."

"Good. That settles that part. There's something else, too." Sally opened her checkbook which she had brought back with the tickets and wrote on one of the slips. She tore out a check and handed it to Tori. "That's two thousand dollars for the charity. I want you to deposit it in your account, and when you're there, make out your own check for that amount."

Tori's mouth hung open as she stared at the check. "I can't take your money. And if I did, why couldn't I just give your check straight to them?"

"Oh, Victoria, don't you see? I'd think it'd be fun for you to whip out your own checkbook. You'll feel like you fit in more. On this, too, I won't take no for an answer."

"Yes, boss." Tori smiled and stuck the check into her purse.

"Great! I knew this was just the thing to cheer you up. Now tell me, how are things going between you and Mr. McKenzie?"

"I guess you can say things are going well. You wouldn't recognize my little place now. He's done a wonderful job."

"Okay, so the situation between your house and him is good, but how about between the two of you?"

"There was a misunderstanding, but it's been straightened out."

"Misunderstanding? Tell your friend Sally all about it." She sat on the couch next to her and patted the her leg.

"It started at David's," she replied, twirling a lock of hair between her fingers and taking a seat. "David left a note. I was upset. Geoff kissed me. Then I treated him like I would a client. He kissed me again. He was apologizing. I was apologizing. Apologizing for two different things we were. Now we're friends."

"He kissed you?"

"Don't make more out of it. He regrets it as it is."

"The nerve of him coming out and saying he regretted doing it," Sally commented with mock seriousness.

"He didn't actually say he regretted it. He said he should have never taken the liberty, and he was sorry."

"Oh."

"Oh?" Tori turned to face Sally and propped an arm on the back of the couch. "Is that all you have to say this time, Ms. Talkative? Oh?"

"Well…" Sally grinned. "You have to admit Geoff is a smart fellow, and smart fellows usually come from good homes with proper upbringings. With proper guidance, you have morals. He was in a dilemma. He's attracted to you. He wanted you. He followed those instincts. Afterwards, his conscience got in the way because it's wrong to hit on a somewhat attached person."

"That makes sense, but I always called David my ex in front of Geoff. And what about me? I was raised right, too, and there I was kissing and wanting to paw Geoff in David's kitchen. Now, here I am getting proposed to by one man and lusting for another."

Sally's bemused smile turned into a full-blown Cheshire cat grin.

"Did I hear right? Did you say *lusting?*"

"I've…" Tori bowed her head hoping to hide the color from the rush of warmth she felt slide to her cheeks. "I've had thoughts."

"I see."

"You see nothing. Here." She held out the two tickets. "Take these back. I can't ask Geoff, and I can't ask David because I don't want to talk to him till I've come to a decision. Therefore, I can't go."

࿄࿅࿄࿅࿄࿅

"You can take them," she said, waving them away. "*And* you can ask Geoff. If he says no, then you've had nothing to worry about. If he says yes, then it may help you to make the right choice. Now go home and get some rest. You have a busy day tomorrow ahead of you."

With her words hanging in the air between them, Sally rose and left the room.

CHAPTER FOURTEEN

*B*usy wasn't the word Tori would have used to describe the morning she had.

She had spent the previous night tossing and turning, her mind and heart warring with each other. Any sleep she had, had only come minutes at a time. Now she could barely keep her eyes open as she listened to the woman on the other end of the line explain what she had been doing when her computer froze.

No food. No sleep. It wasn't a good combination.

"It's really quite simple," Tori said, trying to keep her tongue in check and not say something caustic. It wasn't the lady's fault she couldn't make up her mind about the biggest decision of her life, and that it had kept her awake. It wasn't her client's problem that on top of a couple hours of fitful rest she was ravenous, not having eaten since breakfast the day before. She took a deep breath and counted to ten. "Hit the alt, control and delete buttons at the same time. When the menu screen comes up, select the task manager option. Then on the new screen, click on the program you were using, then click on *end task*. When the next screen comes up asking if you want to wait, don't. Just hit end task again. If that all fails, do the alt-control-delete command, then click on *shut down* and choose *restart*. That will restart and reset your computer, and fix whatever caused the problem."

"But I've done all that already!"

"Have you done a hard shut down and re-started?"

"What's that?" The woman sounded close to tears

"Turn off your computer at the power button."

"No, I haven't."

"Try doing that. Wait about ten to fifteen seconds before you turn it back on. If that still doesn't do the trick, I'll have a technician sent out to you." Her second line rang. Her stomach grumbled. She glanced at the bottom right corner of her monitor. Twelve-thirty, already. "I need to take another call while you do that. I'll be right back."

"Victoria Padden. How may I ser.."

"Victoria. David. Busy?"

"Yes. I have a client on the other line."

"Then I'll make this brief. Though, I did want to continue our discussion."

"Discussion?" She rubbed her sleep-deprived eyes with her thumb and forefinger, blinked, and saw the list of pros and cons she had written sitting in the middle of her clean desk. Oh, that discussion, she thought with disdain.

"Yes, that discussion."

She let out a small gasp. She was more tired than she thought if she spoke her thoughts out loud.

"So, Victoria, what's your answer?"

What was her answer? A surge of panic waved through her body. Line one's *hold* light kept time with her rapidly beating heart. He wanted an answer *now*? Of course he did. Her palms grew moist and slick. Under normal conditions the guy wouldn't even have to wait as long as he had to hear a yes or no to the request. The woman usually had her answer ready the moment the question was popped. Her gaze darted around her cubicle and landed on the sheet of paper. Geoff's name was sprawled all over it.

Damn Sally and damn him. If it weren't for her, she never would have met Geoff. If she had never met Geoff, she'd have a ring on her finger and be making preparations for the big day. If she hadn't met Geoff, she wouldn't be on the receiving end of someone's practical jokes. If she hadn't met him, she wouldn't be more aware of David and his quirks.

If only I had…

"More time."

"Pardon? Did I hear you right? You need more time?"

Her mouth and inner-thoughts had become one. She shook her head and ran her fingers through her hair, wondering when she had formed this weird habit of voicing her thoughts. She did need time, though, so she might as well play along.

"Yes. Give me till Monday."

"Monday? *Monday,*" David shouted the word. "I thought you'd be more receptive to this request. I thought you wanted to get married. Most women when they're proposed to by the man they love and want to spend their life with say yes immediately. They… It's that man, isn't it? You're not being logical because of—"

"David, I am being logical. Getting married is a huge undertaking, a serious matter. A step in a person's life that shouldn't be taken lightly or rushed into. I'm sure most women give ample thought and time to a proposal. They don't accept as readily as you believe. And, they probably say yes right away because the women and their guys talk about it all before hand so both parties are prepared." She shook her head again, amazed how easy the lies had rolled off her tongue. She really needed some sleep. "I'll have an answer for you on Monday."

"But that's four days away."

"David, I have to go. I'll have an answer then." She disconnected the call by pressing the button for line one.

"I'm sorry to—"

"Well, it's about time." The woman's harsh tone echoed over the line. "Your suggestions didn't work. Now all I have is a blue screen. What did you do to my computer? Do you know how much work I have to do? I'm going to lose my job, and it will be all your fault."

৯৮৯৮৯৮৯৬

"Calm down," she stated in a clipped, harsh tone. She hated feeling like everyone was ganging up on her. "It'll be all right. I'll get one of our technicians over there right away. Let me put you on hold so I can—"

"No. Don't you dare put me on hold again. Just get someone over here now!" The distraught woman hung up.

Tori immediately paged the technicians. Only one responded in the allotted fifteen minutes. After she explained the situation to Jim, a good IT representative, but by far not one of the best they had on staff, she slammed the phone down with a heated curse. Jim was not what her client needed, but he was the only one available. All the other technicians were off on calls for Linda. How convenient.

She muttered another curse.

"You're having a wonderful day."

Heat rushed and stole over her face when she heard the familiar deep voice. She glanced up. Geoff stood in the opening of her cubicle, looking at her as if she had grown two heads which were on backwards. She probably did look as awful as that with the lack of sleep, no food, and the habit of mussing up her hair by rubbing her fingers on her head when she was tense. The heat in her cheeks intensified. How much had he heard? She knew her voice had held no warmth or kindness when she had been speaking to Jim, and she had cursed like a sailor.

"How long have you been standing there?"

"Not long. Is everything okay? You look like a haggard old woman with bags under your eyes instead of in your hands."

He had said the awful things with such a teasing lilt in his voice she couldn't come back with a snappy retort or be mad at him for the slights. "You don't know the half of it. I've had a hell of a morning and need a break." A loud gurgle came from her mid-section.

"Sounds like you need food, too," he said with a chuckle. He produced a small bouquet of dried flowers from behind him. "These are for you, but they're not edible, unfortunately."

"Edible or not, they're lovely. Thank you." She laid them down on her desk and picked up the list entitled *Reasons To/Not To Marry David*. She crumpled and tossed the sheet into the wastebasket under her desk.

"The flowers will keep for a long time."

"Yes, they will," she agreed, noticing his gaze was fixed where she had thrown the paper. She didn't think he had seen what was on it. What would she say to him if he had and he brought it up?

Well, Mr. McKenzie, my ex-boyfriend proposed, and I had made up a list of reasons to or not to marry him. As it turns out, because of you, what once would have been an easy yes is becoming a hard no. Because of you, I can't make up my mind.

"So what brings you here?" She moved to the front of her desk to divert his attention away from what she had thrown underneath.

"You." For a moment his gaze was as soft as a caress. He blinked and the look of longing was replaced with puzzlement. "I mean, I came to take you out to lunch."

"My, two lunches in two days. I must be special this week. Hopefully, I'll be able to eat this one."

"What are you talking about?"

"I used my out loud voice again, didn't I?" At his perplexed look, she laughed. "It's nothing. Don't worry about it. I'm tired and hungry, that's all. So where are we going to eat? Not Nespo's, I hope."

"It's a surprise," he answered, still looking confused.

"Okay then. Let me grab my purse."

She bent to retrieve her bag below her desk. The ball of paper had missed its mark. She plucked it from the ground, opened her purse and slipped it in. At least in there she knew it would be safe.

The afternoon sky was a pale blue. Fluffy bunches of white clouds lazily floated overhead. It was a beautiful mild day, perfect for a picnic in the park. Geoff led her over to a private, grassy spot underneath a towering oak tree. It was good to be out in the open, breathing the fresh air. Anything at this point was better than being stuck in a stuffy office. She took a deep cleansing breath and let it out slowly. Bit by bit, her muscles started to relax.

Geoff pulled out a large plaid blanket from the picnic basket he had brought along, grasped two corners, and with a quick flick of his wrists, the sheet billowed out. It fanned gracefully to the ground.

Tori stood and watched as he knelt, pulled out containers, utensils and plates, then two wine glasses and a bottle of white wine.

"Come. Sit down," Geoff said, extending a hand out to her.

"I don't think I should be drinking." She took his hand and found a place on the sheet next to him. "I have to get back to work in a little while."

A husky laugh escaped his throat. "I don't think a couple of glasses will cause any harm. In fact, I think you would need them after the morning you seemed to have had. Besides, you don't have to go back. I saw Sally before I came over to you. Once she heard my plan, she said you could have the rest of the day off. If I remember correctly, her words were, 'Yes, by all means take her,'" he said, raising his voice an octave. "'Explain to her what happens to Jill with all work and no play.'"

"You're impression of her isn't so hot, but I believe you. She'd say that. You're right. A glass won't hurt. Pour away."

He opened the bottle and poured them each a glass. As Tori sipped on the wine, she watched him open the containers and fix their plates. He produced her favorite picnic food items. First came a creamy cucumber salad followed by potato salad, then a piece of baked chicken. Around the rim of the plate, he placed some fresh strawberries, pieces of melon and grapes. Her heart caught in her throat and she stared in disbelief. David had never done anything like this for her. In the couple of years they had been together, he had never presented her with a lunch consisting of her favorite foods. Here was this man, this wonderful, thoughtful man, whom she barely knew, doing it.

He didn't make her decision easier, that was for sure.

"Here you go. A feast fit for a queen."

She balanced the wine glass next to her and reached out for the plate. "How did you know what I would like?"

"Let me just say a little birdie told me."

"Would the birdie's name be Sally?"

He winked and shared in her laughter.

As he focused on his plate of food, she took a moment to study him. Why he wasn't involved with anyone perplexed her. He wasn't ugly, just the opposite. He was very handsome. His dark, thick hair and his chocolate brown eyes could make a woman weak in the knees. She knew that from experience. Then there was the way he carried himself, proud and sure, taking command of situations. He possessed intelligence and a witty sense of humor, too. Why wouldn't a woman want him?

They ate in companionable silence, and she watched his big hands maneuver the small plate and fork. Such strong fingers. They would work wonders with a kink in the neck or back, or bring pleasure to an assortment of other areas. She popped a strawberry in her mouth to stifle a giggle. It didn't work.

"And what's that snigger for?"

"I was thinking." She racked her mind in search of something quick and witty to say. "If Mrs. Sims had her way, it could be Bertha sitting here with you instead of me."

"Heaven forbid," Geoff groaned. "I'd have to make enough food to feed a small army."

࿊࿊࿊࿊࿊࿊

Laughter bubbled forth from both of them, and once she had caught her breath, she asked, "So what's the deal between you and them, anyway?"

"Mrs. Sims is husband hunting for her daughter. For years now, they have tried to get her with every known eligible business man between Philly and New York."

"That's a lot of men."

"Yes, it is, and luckily, I had been successful in hiding from them even with Mr. Sims being one of my biggest clients. My downfall came two years ago when the paper did an article on the area's most eligible bachelors. I did an interview."

"I remember that. David had been called, too, but he declined." She cringed at Geoff's scowl at the mention of David's name. "Sorry. Go on."

"Anyway, when Mrs. Sims realized I worked for her husband and was a very local and very eligible bachelor, she set her sights on me and hasn't let up since. Even Bertha got into the swing of it."

"So why don't you placate them with a couple of dates, then break it off?"

"It's not that simple." Geoff ran his fingers through his thick mass of hair. "With these two it's all or nothing. If I were to go out with her, it would be a short matter of time before word got around that we're an item. Then, if I were to break it off, it could ruin my business or reputation or both."

"How so?"

"Mrs. Sims is a very influential woman and the head of what's considered the gossip chain in this area. She'd be able to slander my name and create vicious lies without batting an eye. The sad part is people would believe her. They would take her word over mine. I don't want to take any chances."

"I understand."

"Besides, what man would want a thirty year old, whiney, spoiled brat—"

"Who throws tantrums and probably sucks her thumb—"

Laughter rained between them, seeming to brighten the already beautiful surroundings. In the process, their gazes caught each other's and held fast.

"I'm happy to see you in a good mood." His voice was low and husky, and when he brought his hand toward her face, the laughter caught in her throat. "You seemed out of sorts back at your office."

"Yes, I was a bit off this morning, but it's nothing a little food and some sleep can't cure." The backs of his fingers grazed her cheek. She leaned into the touch. "Do you know what would make my mood even better?"

"What?" he asked, placing a lock of hair behind her ear.

"If you'd say you'd go with me to the Children's Charity Banquet and Ball tomorrow night."

* * * *

He jerked his hand away from her face so abruptly, she jerked back, too. He couldn't help his reaction. Her innocent request brought forth memories he thought he had buried deep long ago.

"Geoff? What? I'm sorry. Maybe I shouldn't have asked." She turned her face away.

What was it his cousin had said? *If you don't let them into your world, how are you going to carry on any kind of relationship?* He had to tell her. She deserved to know his wife had volunteered her time with that same charity.

Gently, he took hold of her chin and turned her face back to his.

"It's not that I don't want to go with you. What you said just brought back unpleasant memories."

"Oh. If you don't want to go, I understand."

"Let me explain why first." He hated seeing that naked look of hurt in her eyes, but he had to go on. "My wife used to volunteer for that charity."

"Wife?" She yanked her chin out of his hand and scooted away. "Did you say wife?"

ᔔᦥᔔᦥᔔᦥ

"Tori?" He inched toward her, and she inched away, so he stopped. "Tori, listen to me before you get more hysterical. She's my ex-wife now. Ex. I haven't seen her in about fifteen years."

Her eyes widened. She bobbed her head once with a quiet, "Go on."

That acknowledgment was all the encouragement he needed to continue. "When I first began my business, I went to school at night. Sue Ellen and I rarely saw each other. To keep herself busy, she donated her evenings to the charity. I had no problems with that just as I thought she had no problems with my foundling business and college course load. She never complained we weren't together enough. Though, the few times she did, she said when we were together she felt like a sex toy." At Tori's downcast look at his last remark, he decided not to expound on it. No one really ever cared to hear about their significant other's conquests no matter how open or honest the relationship, did they? "I thought she could see the future as I could, that everything I did worked toward our being with each other more. I guess I had put blinders on and made myself believe she was happy when she wasn't. After about a year, it happened…" He paused, remembering all too well the night he had arrived home to find it empty of her things and how he reacted to her leaving him with a fit of uncontrolled anger which destroyed a lot of furniture.

"What happened?"

"She left. She walked out of our marriage. I wasn't even home. I thought she had been out at the charity function. I had told her earlier in the day I'd be staying after class to talk to my professor so I'd be late. I gather she figured it was her opportunity to leave. When I got home, I found her note. She had written she was leaving me. She wasn't coming back. It'd be useless for me to try and find her. Her last words were that she'd be in touch." A shudder racked his body as he recalled the hurt, the anger, the pain he had experienced that night. He had lost part of his sanity. He felt an arm go over his shoulders.

"I did try to find her," he continued. "But without luck. A few months later, I was served with divorce papers. The firm she had hired was out of New York City. I tried everything to make them let me contact her. They wouldn't budge. I signed the papers. The divorce was easy. She didn't want anything. She divorced me on grounds of estrangement—hers. I haven't heard from her since."

"Sounds like you really loved her. Perhaps you still do?"

"No, once upon a time I loved her. People said we had gotten married too young, that it wouldn't work. I wanted to prove them wrong. I would have given her the sun, moon, and stars if she had waited."

"Perhaps you'll find someone again."

"Maybe…" He turned his head and their gazes locked.

* * * *

A quick intake of breath whistled through her teeth and a tremor rippled through her. Without breaking their gaze, he lowered his head and touched his lips to hers.

A light breeze drifted by carrying the soft sound of music playing in the distance. With her senses heightened by his slow and thoughtful kiss, she heard a woman sing about commitment. Commitment and love. David and Geoff. A brief shiver ran through her. Was kissing him wrong since a proposal still hung between her and her David? Proposal or not, Lord help her, the kiss felt so right.

His kiss became more persuasive. She met his command by parting her lips and letting him taste her. The meeting of their mouths was like nothing she had ever enjoyed with David. Geoff nicked her lips with his teeth, caressing her tongue with his. Warmth blanketed her body and enveloped her spirit. His kiss wasn't chaste or inexperienced as Jack's had been. Nor bland and practiced, as if he had the right to kiss her because he was a man and she a woman, like David's had been. Geoff brought her desires and passion out, making her feel alive and sensual. When his hand moved from her chin to cup the back of her head and his arm wrapped around her, she was grateful for the support. He was like the sun to her, making her world warm and happy.

He laid her down on the picnic blanket and trailed a hand down the front of her body. Over her clothes, he massaged her breast, passing his thumb over her nipple several times, bringing it to a hard nub beneath her bra. Passionate need hammered at her common sense. Her logic flew the coop of her mind and she pushed her chest into his hand, giving silent permission for him to play while she sucked on his lower lip.

Apparently taking the hint, Geoff's hand moved to the bottom of her shirt. He inched his warm fingers between her top and her skin, creating searing paths of pleasure as they traveled up and slipped under her bra. His heated palm cupped her breast, then caressed the mound. Sensations she hadn't felt in ages flooded her body. The last time she'd done something daring with a man outside, she'd been with Steve. Those were thoughts that she didn't want to entertain while Geoff's warm palm caressed her skin.

Surrendering to the restlessness inside her and not caring should anyone come upon them, she nipped his tongue. A fleeting thought ran through her head. *You keep this up, Geoff, I'll no doubt say no to David and fall in love with you.*

No sooner did her silent statement end, the kiss stopped. She lay on the ground for a moment with her eyes closed, savoring the lingering traces of his lips on her body, the dainty breeze teasing the moist areas of her mouth.

"You're like no other woman I've ever met," he murmured near her ear.

"I should tell you David's asked me to marry him." Her eyelids flew open as the words quietly tumbled out. She stared at Geoff, biting her lower lip, praying he wouldn't flip out too badly.

The hooded look of longing in Geoff's eyes darkened. "And your answer was?" he asked smoothly. His expression turned unreadable.

"I told him I needed time to think. I'm to have an answer for him on Monday."

"Good." He straightened her shirt, then sat up. "I wouldn't want to take another man's fiancée to a ball."

"Ball?" She sat up, adjusting her undergarment, then smoothing her shirt.

"Yes, ball." The cold, hard look he gave her wasn't what she expected. "You know. You asked me out. I'm accepting."

"Oh, yes, right. I had forgotten." Heat rushed to her cheeks and to the roots of her hair.

Geoff smiled devilishly.

They both knew why she had forgotten.

He took hold of her upper arm, looking as if he wanted to say something, when his cell phone rang. He released her, unclipped it from his belt and looked at the number.

"Damn. It's my office." He let it go to voicemail.

"We should get going, anyway," she said in a hesitant voice, rising and stepping off the blanket, feeling awkward about what had transpired between them and bothered by his mood swing. "I need to make a stop before I get back to work. It's a good thing I suggested taking two vehicles, isn't it?"

He grumbled a reply she couldn't catch as he wrapped everything in the blanket and shoved it into the basket. His surly attitude didn't lessen as they walked over to the parking lot. At her car, he gave her a quick hard kiss on her cheek.

"I'll pick you up at seven."

After he jumped into his truck and tore out of the parking lot, she made her way over to David's house.

Paperwork was strewn about his desk. Out of habit, she straightened it up, telling herself she did it so he'd be able to find her payment for her expenses. She wrote out the check with relief. She would never have to do that again, married or not. As she placed it down, she noticed a long white envelope had fallen to the floor. Her heart skipped a beat. Was it him? Was he actually the one sending her the unnerving notes? Breathing so she wouldn't completely freak out, she bent to retrieve it and told herself she was being silly. She had already figured out David wasn't behind the letters she had received. A glance at the return address stated it was from a man named Lynden Coors, and it was addressed to David at Valley View. She placed the unopened piece of mail on the desk.

On the way to her car, she heard a man's curse coming from the direction of the garage. Had she missed David when she was inside? She walked over to the garage door and was about to call out to him when she heard him inside swearing. With her ear to the door, she could barely make out what he was saying, but was able to discern that he was on the phone.

"Damn it, didn't you just hear me? I said you're not supposed to call me on my private lines. No, even as a patient you're not supposed to. Well, if it's an emergency, then you call the office and they'll patch you through to the doctor on call. I'm flattered you want me as your counselor but…no…I said no. Call my office and book an appointment. Yes, I proposed to my girlfriend. You know what? This conversation is over. Goodbye."

David growled and utter some more expletives, then a crash of tools clattered on the concrete garage floor. Assuming he had thrown something or pushed something over, she hurried to her car. There was no way she wanted to be caught outside and have to deal with another man's foul mood.

Tori's spirits sank notch by notch as she drove back to work. What was David doing talking to patients at home, especially in that manner? Was he that stressed?

With one hand on the steering wheel, she used the other to massage the top of her head. She couldn't deal with a

ೊ෧ೊ෧ೊ෧

headache, not right now. The lack of a good night's rest and the circumstances at the picnic had taken their toll. She no longer wanted to deal with anyone's drama.

CHAPTER FIFTEEN

"*T*hat's not a reason! Not a reason at all!" Linda stood on a chair yelling her complaints down to everyone.

When Tori stepped into the office, utter chaos reigned.

A handful of office workers stood in a pack laughing, tears streaming down their faces, while others chased a fury little animal around the cubicles. Sally stood apart from it all with a smug expression on her face, occasionally adding a laugh of her own.

Tori made her way over to Sally, dodging the on-lookers. She almost tripped over Snowpea as the small dog barreled around corner and darted by her feet.

"Seems like Snowpea's having a grand ol' time." She gestured in the direction of the animal and laughing as he eluded another person.

Sally stopped laughing the moment Tori spoke. "Actually, it had been quite peaceful until recently. Snowpea had been with me all day and hadn't caused one lick of trouble. Then all hell broke loose. I had to deal with two phone calls back to back with very irate clients just as Linda had come in and screamed bloody murder. Snowpea, not realizing he had been the cause of her distress, started running about looking for the danger. He kept going to Linda because she was the one screaming. She's dancing. He's prancing. She jumped up on the chair and let out another shriek. Snowpea raced again. Then the others had joined in the chase. If Linda," Sally raised her voice to be heard over the din in the office, "would stop screaming, Snowpea would stop running."

"Get that thing out of here," Linda yelled, pointing to the dog running circles around the chair. Every time she opened her mouth and spoke, the dog yelped.

No wonder the poor little pooch is frightened, Victoria mused.

The tall, redhead was probably huge to the tiny dog. On a chair, she'd be a giant. Plus, her high-pitched ranting could cut through bone.

"My Snowpea is not a thing," Sally retorted curtly. She hunched down and crooned, "Come here, darling. It's all right. Come to Momma."

In a flash, the dog was in her arms and she stood.

"It's okay, baby. The big brute won't hurt you. You've had enough excitement for one day. We'll go home in a little while and have a treat." Sally crooned to the dog as she went into her private office. The dog yipped in pleasure. Sally slammed her door.

"There should be a law about bringing animals into an office," Linda remarked as she stomped from the chair onto the floor. She straightened her dress and the silk scarf around her neck.

"Chill out," said Sean.

Linda gave the intern a heated glare and stormed away.

Tori shook her head. What a day this turned out to be. She couldn't wait until it was over.

It wasn't long before Linda found Tori at her desk. "So who's the guy who brought you the flowers?"

Tori looked up from her interns' and Jim's reports. "Not that it's any of your business, Linda, but they're from a friend."

"A friend, eh? Isn't that nice. I thought…"

Tori waited for Linda to continue. The woman traced her finger around the tape dispenser. She lost her battle with her patience and wanted to strangle Linda with the garment the garish redhead wore around her neck.

"You thought what?"

"Oh, nothing." Linda removed her hand and leaned over the desk. "I guess since you're still here, Sally didn't say anything."

Tori cringed at the wicked grin and gleam in Linda's eye.

"Sally explained what had happened before I came back. Never knew you were afraid of tiny little dogs that couldn't hurt flies, Linda." She was satisfied with her barb when the smile left her co-worker's face.

"That's not what I was referring to," Linda huffed. "Sally told me to tell you she wants to see you in her office. Oh, and Tori, though she appears happy, she's not. She's not pleased at all."

* * * *

Geoff wasn't in high spirits. He had raced back to the office only to find the place deserted. Then he had spent the next half hour calling around to the sites to locate Philip and see what had prompted the emergency call.

He had just ended a lengthy conversation with Mr. Sims when Philip, looking as if he hadn't a care in the world, sauntered into the office with a coffee cup in one hand and a magazine in the other. His hair wasn't in disarray and his eyes were clear and focused. From his cousin's calm appearance, Geoff knew there had been no cause for alarm.

If he wasn't annoyed before, he was now. He had planned to spend his afternoon with Tori and now his time with her was ruined for nothing.

"Hey, cuz. Looks like something's eating you."

"What was the emergency?" Geoff said, using all his strength to keep his anger in check.

"Emergency?" Philip placed his coffee and magazine on the desk, then sat on the edge of it. "What gave you the idea there was an emergency?"

"Don't play innocent with me, cousin. You may be family, but I can still fire your ass."

"Fire me?" Phil jumped from the desk and backed away. "What the hell has gotten into you?"

"What's gotten into me? What's gotten into you? If there wasn't an emergency, you better have a good excuse for leaving me that—" Geoff stopped talking as Phil laughed. "What's so funny?"

"You."

Geoff frowned at him.

"No, I don't mean you. I mean… I…" Laughter choked off his words.

"Out with it!"

"I'm sorry." Philip took a deep breath to still his mirth. "Yes, you did say only to page or call you if something dire happened, but you've also said to do it if you were out on a date. Let me see. How'd it go? 'I have to seem important. I have to make them believe my business is my priority and it's successful, very successful. So whenever I'm out on a date, after a reasonable amount of time, page me. Not only will they believe I'm the man I claim to be, but it will cut the date short so I don't have to get involved too much.' Did I get it right?"

Speechless, Geoff dropped his jaw. Where his cousin got his strange memory from, he had no idea. "That was years ago when I had just started to make headway. You haven't used that trick in ages."

"You haven't dated in ages, either. When you told me this morning you planned on taking Victoria out, I figured the rule was still in effect since you hadn't told me different. I was only following orders, boss." He saluted Geoff. "So, you still gonna fire me?"

"No." Geoff leaned back in his chair and stared up at the ceiling. He had forgotten all about that stupid pact he had made with Philip. All his dates ended with the familiar sound, sometimes an hour into them, sometimes longer. One time Phil had ended a date of his fifteen minutes into it. When he had found him later and asked why he had done it so quickly, his cousin had shrugged and said he hadn't like her.

In retrospect, he hadn't needed any help in not getting too involved with the women. They always took care of ending the relationships.

"No," Geoff repeated. "I'm not going to fire you. Maybe I'll just lock you in a closet for a while." He couldn't help but smile when he saw Philip's eyes bulge.

"You wouldn't."

"Don't tempt me."

"I guess your date with her was going well when I interrupted."

Geoff nodded.

"So when do I get to meet her?"

"I don't know."

"You don't know. Is that more of a yes, eventually I'll meet the girl who's put the light back in your eyes and a spring in your step? Or more of a no, she's not the meet the family type girl?"

"She might be getting married."

"Married?" Coffee spritzed out of his mouth.

Geoff wiped his shoulder although Phil's spittle had come nowhere near him.

"Yes, to some doctor, or actually soon-to-be doctor. She hasn't given him an answer yet. She and I are going to a charity ball tomorrow night. Hopefully the date will help her decide."

"That's strange." Phil rubbed his chin and focused on a point outside the window.

"What is?" Geoff turned to see what might have been happening outside behind him that caught his cousin's attention. He watched the wind carry a stray piece of newspaper away. "I don't see anything."

"Of course not. I wasn't referring to outside, but to Victoria."

"There is," Geoff said with a low growl of protectiveness, leaning over the desk and glaring at Phil, "nothing strange about her and I would suggest you mind what words come out of your mouth concerning her."

"Not her. Her reaction." Phil raised his hands for peace. "Most women I know would say yes right off the bat. I've listened to Steph and her friends enough times to know if I were to pop the question, there'd be no hesitation on her part. Or any of her friends if I were to ask one of them." He chuckled and winked. "And gauging your reaction, I'd say you're in love with Victoria."

Geoff's head snapped up as if he had been given an uppercut to the chin. "You're wrong, and again, watch your mouth."

"Now you sound like my mom."

Before Geoff's could make contact, Phil smiled and jumped for the door.

"The hell I'm wrong," Phil muttered and closed the door behind him.

Geoff sank back into his chair. Love? No. He hardly knew the woman. Sure, she was one of the most beautiful women he had ever been attracted to. She was funny, intelligent and so sexy when her temper flared. Stubborn, too, but he liked that. Tori wouldn't bend under pressure. He couldn't wait to see her again. See her smile. Hear her laugh. But in love with her? So soon? Ridiculous.

He put his head in his hands. What was absurd was how his heart felt empty and heavy when he thought he could lose her to another man before they would even have a chance together.

He'd have to remedy that. And, when better to start than tomorrow night at the ball?

He picked up the phone to call in a favor.

* * * *

"Linda said you wanted to see me," Tori said, uneasy about what was to come.

"Yes, I do. Come in, shut the door and have a seat." Sally didn't take her gaze off her computer.

Her friend didn't seem like her normal self. No smiles of greeting welcomed her. Her lips were straight-laced, tight, without warmth. She had an air of anxiousness and tenseness about her, not the relaxed, *everything's all right* poise Tori had come to know. Sally acted like a very irritated and stressed boss.

With apprehension, she took her place in a chair across the desk from Sally and braced for the wrath she had only heard about from others. Sally finished typing and faced her. The fiery, angry look in Sally's eyes made her flinch.

"If it were anyone, *anyone* else, sitting in front of me right now, I'd be handing them a pink slip and sending them packing." Sally's words boomed against the walls of the room. She took a deep breath. "Since this concerns you, though, I am going against what I normally preach so consider yourself lucky."

Tori sat paralyzed to the chair. *What have I done?*

"As I told you, I had received two very upsetting phone calls earlier. Due to my diplomacy, or the fact these companies don't have the time to search for new technicians, I was able to sort out the problems and keep them as our clients. The first call was from Mrs. Hadley. She said you were rude and condescending to her this morning. That you put her on hold for an exorbitant amount of time. That you sent over a very inept technician. Is this correct? No explanations for the moment. A simple yes or no will suffice." Sally rose and strolled over to the large picture window.

She wanted to explain, to make her friend understand the sleepless night she had, the reason for putting the woman on hold, the reason for sending Jim. Most of all she wanted to placate her boss. "Yes."

"I have also told you your interns' actions reflect on you and you are responsible for any errors they cause. Is this correct?" The woman closed the blinds and returned to her desk.

"Yes." Tori felt as big as an ant under Sally's scrutiny. She bowed her head.

"The second call was from Mr. Duphrey at Greentree. Seems some of the representatives were on the Internet and all their computers have picked up a virus. Their computers are useless to them now. They had to close down for the day. They're losing money because of this. Did you, or did you not say, the firewalls were put up?"

"I did."

"Well, they didn't work. Obviously Sid and Keith don't know what they're doing. I have Sunil and Ed over there right now to undo the damage. I had to use every ounce of my persuasion to make them believe you hadn't deliberately bugged their system. Now that I've hidden us from prying eyes, you want to tell me what's going on?"

Tori kept her head down. A warm tear trickled down her cheek. If only Geoff hadn't gotten that call. She might have been able to do damage control if she'd been here. "David's been after me. I haven't been sleeping well." She paused, wondering if she should mention the letters and phone calls. Sally knew about her issues with Steve, her subsequent paranoia, but she didn't have anything concrete and didn't want to worry her when it was obvious Sally had much more on her mind. "I'm feeling anxious about being back at my place which isn't helping matters any."

"Steve's still away, right?"

"As far as I know."

Sally sat back, crossed her arms over her stomach. "I'm sorry you're under stress, Tori, but you know how I feel about employees bringing personal issues to work and letting them interfere with their jobs. You also know I have to do something, or else the rest of my employees will feel I've softened, or worse yet, played favorites. Since I'm not going to fire you, I'm relieving you of the new accounts and lowering your pay back to what it was before you took them over. Your last act for Greentree will be to go over there and help right the wrong. Once that's done, go home and take tomorrow off. Okay?"

"Yes." Numb, Tori rose, keeping her focus averted from Sally and made it to the door.

"You understand my…my position, don't you?" Sally's voice hitched behind her.

"Yes." She had worked hard to please others, making herself into someone her friends and family could be proud of. For what? Nothing, it now seemed. She kept her hand on the doorknob and didn't turn around, not wanting Sally to see the tears of humiliation coursing down her face.

"I really didn't need this today," Sally continued. "I figured I'd have time to cool off since you were supposed to be with Geoff the rest of the afternoon. Those two calls… Frank has to have surgery. Linda's demanding more accounts and money. And you, my pride and joy. Have a good time at the ball. We'll talk Saturday."

Tori hurried from the room, viciously wiping the tears from her eyes with the backs of her hands. When she reached her desk, she grabbed several tissues and patted her skin.

"Oh, how the mighty have fallen," Linda cackled from a few cubicles away.

Tori grabbed her purse, strengthened her resolve, and with her head held high, left the building.

Mr. Duphrey, Mrs. Evans and Mr. Tarran coldly greeted Tori at the door when she arrived at Greentree, and without words, they led her down to the basement.

She greeted Ed and Sunil while ignoring the trio's icy stares, and asked her associates for a progress report. They explained after questioning all the employees, they had found the virus had come in through an online game.

"Game? My employees are playing games?" Mr. Tarran directed his questions to Mr. Duphrey.

"Max assured me he was on break," Mr. Duphrey replied, turning red around his collar.

"As I was saying," Sunil continued, "it was an online game that has multiple players. One of the players must have had the virus and transmitted it during a strategic maneuver. When Max went to retaliate, his screen went black and a box appeared requesting a pass code. Since all the computers are networked and the virus was a tricky bastard, all the towers got hit."

Tori sat down and looked at the screen in front of her. The display read *What's the Magic Word(s)?* Underneath the question beat a large cursor.

"We've been at it over an hour trying to break the code," added Ed.

Why me? What have I done to deserve this? A light clicked on in her mind. *Why me, indeed.* On a whim, she typed in her name and hit *enter.* There was no explanation as to why or how the person or persons who sent her the threatening messages would go this far, but then again nothing in her life seemed to make any sense anymore.

The question disappeared. She heard a few gasps behind her.

"At least she's making progress," Ed's awed voice murmured.

The screen came back up. *Good try. What's the Magic Word(s)?*

Determined to make more headway, she typed in her whole name.

Try again. What's the Magic Word(s)?

She typed in Cease.

Close. Try again. What's the Magic Word(s)?

Her fingers flew over the keys. CeaseandDesist.

BINGO!

The computer screen went back to normal. She found her way into the heart of the server to locate the programming and histories. With lightning speed, she went from screen to screen, noticing none of the components had been damaged. She began a trace of the address where the virus came from. A couple more histories and the screen went black.

"Damn, it happened again," came Mr. Duphrey's voice from behind. "You call yourself a computer tech?"

She was about to turn around and give him a piece of her mind, when she noticed the screen change into a hodgepodge of letters.

Now what was her friend *trying to say?*

She relaxed her eyes and took in the whole page.

The message was sporadically placed, reminding her of the Armageddon bible code show she had watched on television but it was there, nonetheless.

IT'S NOT A VIRUS. JUST A BUG TO GET YOUR ATTENTION. YOU MADE A HUGE MISTAKE. YOU CAN'T RUN AND YOU CAN'T HIDE. I   CAN TRACK YOU WITH EASE. FOLLOW YOU WHEREEVER YOU GO. MAKE YOUR LIFE HELL.

She thought hard about the messages and the people in her life, trying to figure out who would do this. Steve wasn't smart enough to hack into a system and leave her a message. David and Geoff didn't have the skills either. A shiver racked her body as a realization settled in her mind. *Not another stalker.* Her stomach dropped and her skin prickled. But this time she didn't know who the person was, which made the situation much worse. How was she going to tell the authorities about this now? When things went south with Steve, she'd had concrete proof and a person to hand over to the cops and they couldn't do anything until it was almost too late. Now all she had was some icky feelings, notes she could have typed up on a computer and a few prank-like calls that even she hadn't been able to trace. Her life seemed to be in danger again, and there was nothing she could do to stop the looming threats.

With a sigh, she executed a keyboard command. The page printed out and the standard desktop appeared. It might not be much as evidence but eventually every little bit would count…when the authorities were fishing her body out of a river or some other dumping ground for murder victims…

"So?" Mr. Duphrey inquired, breaking her from the thoughts of her demise at the hands of a madman or woman.

"Ed, Sunil, run some diagnostics. I didn't see any damage, but it's better to be safe than sorry. I don't believe it was a virus, just a very bad prank some hacker played. But check anyway."

"Nothing but letters," Mrs. Evans said, studying the print out. "Like someone was trying to learn to type and not doing a good job of it."

"I'm sure it's nothing." Tori snatched the paper out of her hand. "I wanted to print it out so my office can analyze it. See if there's some kind of pattern."

"Oh. Okay."

"Mr. Tarran, Mr. Duphrey, the problem seems to be solved. I do suggest you tell your employees that unless it's work related they should stay off the Net." She nodded to her co-workers and they began running the tests.

"Now if you'll excuse me." Tori put her latest warning in her purse and left the basement.

Even knowing that they couldn't help her, she had to go to the police and for that she'd need to get her courage up.

She also had to stop seeing Geoff, lest he get caught in the middle of the bizarre incidents of letters and phone calls and get hurt.

Tomorrow night would be soon enough to cross that hurdle with him.

CHAPTER SIXTEEN

*T*he pile of clothes lay on the bed like a grotesque blob of colors, taunting Tori to make a decision out of its mess. She had been in the process of a decision for what seemed like an eternity, trying to find the right thing to wear to the ball, the right thing to wear when she told Geoff they couldn't see each other anymore.

Had she been at work earlier, the final choice would have been easy. She would have had to rush home, and under the pressure of time, would have had to make a quick decision. Tori would have been able to ask Sally her opinion. She could call her, but Sally had made it all too clear she didn't want to talk to her for a couple of days.

Now she stood in front of an empty closet with too much time on her hands. She had even slept in and taken her time getting to the task of her search. The postponement hadn't helped. There were still four hours left until Geoff picked her up. Too much time to think and let her mind keep changing course. The blue V-neck suit or her favorite evening gown? David or Geoff? To be overdressed or underdressed? Geoff or David?

Realizing she finally had to be truthful with herself, she paused in her search. There wasn't much of a choice. David had turned into a total drip and needed to go. But she had to let Geoff go, too. Could she deal with being on her own right now? She shook her head, not wanting to think about the impending break up.

So, what to wear? She, of all people, should know the answer. Then again, her mother had always told her what to

᪥᪥᪥᪥᪥᪥

wear, not the reason why. She slapped her forehead with the heel of her hand.

"Why didn't I think of that before?"

She raced into her office and picked up her phone to call her mother.

There was no dial tone. No sound at all coming through. *No, not today, not now of all times!*

"Hello? Hello? Anyone there?" A woman's voice came from the handset.

"Mom?"

"Victoria?"

She sank down to her knees next to her desk, grateful it wasn't another prank, wasn't something worse.

"Hi, Mom. I was just about to call you."

"Well, I saved you the dime. I must say that was the quickest I've ever had someone answer. I didn't even hear it ring."

"Neither did I. What a coincidence we were thinking of each other at the same time. So what can I do for you? Or did you just call to say hello?"

"I'll tell you in a moment. What I want to know first is why my daughter thought of calling me."

Tori explained her predicament about the attire for the evening.

"I'd wear the evening gown, darling. Rather be stunning than embarrassed. Funny, David didn't mention anything about taking you out to a formal affair this evening."

"David?"

"Yes. He and I had a nice chat this morning. That's why I'm calling. I tried to reach you at work, but they told me you weren't there. Now, Victoria, you'll tell me what's going on. Why are you stringing the poor man along? I thought you wanted to marry him, marry a doctor. And what's this with you not being at work? The woman who told me you were out seemed quite pleased about your absence and mentioned something about a demotion."

Linda. Tori fumed. Linda had no idea how close she came to being put in the hospital.

"Oh, Mom, the past few days have been hell." Her mother gasped over her language, but Tori continued on. "There were a couple of problems with some of our clients at work, and instead of firing me, Sally took away my new accounts. It's nothing a few months of hard work won't be able to fix. I'm not in today because she said I could have the day off. As for the function, I'm not going with David. I didn't invite him."

"You didn't invite him? Then who, may I ask, are you going with?"

"His name is Geoff. I believe I've told you about him. He's—"

"The construction worker?" her mother inquired with an inflection of revulsion, followed by a sharp intake of breath.

"He's not a construction worker. Well, he is in a sense, but he owns the company. He's a nice guy, Mom. You'd like him. Dad would like him, too. Geoff reminds me a lot of him— kind, strong, handsome…"

"I don't like the sound of this," Felicia stated in a short cold tone.

"The sound of what?"

"'Kind, strong, handsome'," her mother mimicked in a silky voice. "Sounds like you're smitten with him."

"Smitten? Smitten? Who says that nowadays?"

"You shouldn't entertain any kind of thoughts toward the man. What would your fiancé think?"

"He's not my fiancé, Mother," Tori replied tersely, not appreciating her mother's assumption. "I don't know that he will be. I'm beginning to believe he's not the one for me."

"It's that man, isn't it?"

"You've talked to David for too long because you sound like him now." Tori sighed. "No, it's not Geoff. There've been problems between David and me for a while." She paused. "I want to thank you, Mom."

"Thank me for what?"

"For telling me what to wear."

"Well, you're welcome for the clothing advice. I only hope you'll make the right choice when it comes to David. I don't want to be disappointed. Bye, dear."

Tori looked at the silent phone in her hand.

A short while later she had all her clothes put away and her evening gown hanging in the bathroom. Around five, she planned to take a shower which, at the same time, would steam the few wrinkles out of the dress. Then she'd do her hair and make-up and don her outfit last. By the time she was done, she wouldn't have to wait long until Geoff picked her up.

What if he came in his truck? She nervously paced about her bedroom, the question ringing in her head. How would she manage getting in and out of that vehicle in a gown? Should she reconsider her apparel again? No, she'd make do. She was, after all, a resourceful, intelligent woman who could think her way through any problem. Now it was a question of heels or flats. She stood with her hands on her hips staring at the pile of footwear at the bottom of the closet.

Her doorbell rang.

"Victoria Padden?" a cheerful mailman greeted her.

"Yes?"

"I have a package you need to sign for, as well as your mail, and I found this taped to your door."

She balanced the parcels in her arms and signed for the overnight delivery.

"Have a good day, ma'am." He turned on his heel and left.

She eyed the blank white envelope warily as she made her way over to the couch and dumped the contents of her arms onto the coffee table. Good news or bad news first? First the bad. It could always be softened with the good afterwards.

She tore open the envelope and pulled out a photograph of her at the park getting into her car. A black *X* crossed out her head. She flipped the picture over.

STOP SEEING HIM OR ELSE.

A small cry escaped her throat. Who was doing this to her, to them? If she only knew, she could tell them to stop, tell them tonight would be her last time with Geoff. All she wanted was one real date with him and then it would be over. Was that too much to ask for?

No, it wasn't. What harm could come to anyone because two adults decided to be friends and go out together? There had to be thousands of males and females in the world who enjoyed each other's company without them being construed as a romantic couple. Why should her relationship with Geoff be any different?

To be on safe side, though, she'd still tell him she couldn't see him anymore. She'd tell him at the banquet instead of after, like she had planned. There would be witnesses. Word would get back to whomever it was who plagued her and the horrible, frightening messages would stop.

Then maybe her life would return to normal.

She set the picture aside and opened the small package. The brown paper came away easily and revealed a box that had Geoff's work address on it. She pried the tape loose with her fingernail. Nestled within amongst newspaper padding was a thin, rectangular one. Inside the smaller box, laid a string of pearls and underneath them a small card.

Hope these will go with what you are planning to wear. Till tonight, Geoff.

No. She definitely would *not* call off her date.

"Damn it, not again." Victoria swore a few hours later as she pulled a third pair of ripped panty hose from her legs. She threw the ruined garment into the wastebasket in the bathroom with the others and went in search for some more. Her drawers came up empty.

☙◆❧◆☙◆❧

"Where'd all my hose go, for crying out loud?"

She spied her hamper and realized they were all in the wash.

She eyed her clock. Six forty-five. There was no time to do laundry or run to the store for a new pair. She'd have to go bare. Several knocks at the door interrupted her trek back to the bathroom. She clutched her bathrobe closed under her neck and swung the door open.

"You look…"

The look of astonishment on Geoff's face, the canned compliment he'd almost completed, and the fact she wanted to look her best when he picked her up and failed at it, riled her irritation even more. "Not one word, Mr. McKenzie. As you can see, I'm not having a pleasant evening so far and any comments from the peanut gallery will not be appreciated."

"So I've gathered," he replied with a suppressed chuckle. From behind his back, he pulled forward his left hand and waved a package of panty hose. "I'll give you what's hidden behind my back in my other hand when you're done dressing."

Joy bubbled in her as she took the gift from him. She'd be especially careful with these when she put them on. She looked up at him with gratitude in her eyes. "How?"

He put up his empty hand to stop her question from going any further. "I have a sister. She always needed these things at the last moment. I hope they fit."

"I'm sure they will," she answered, clutching the thin package to her chest. "Have a seat. I'll be out shortly." She ran into the bathroom.

* * * *

When she reappeared, Geoff rose on trembling legs. She looked stunning. His heart beat erratically as he drank in the sight of her. The long black gown clung to her body accentuating the dips and curves of her figure. The neckline swept low, and he found himself gazing at her breasts rounded up from the tight fitting bodice. The movement of her fingers stroking the pearls he had sent diverted his attention from her chest. He swallowed hard, met her gaze and held out his second gift.

"This is for you," he choked out. He felt like a nervous eighteen-year-old going to the prom. How could he help it when she looked so beautiful? Her hair and makeup had been done when she had answered the door, but her bathrobe had distracted him from how pretty its effects were. Now that she was dressed, he was overwhelmed. Her wavy hair, pinned up in a chignon, had thin curly tendrils along the sides of her head. The soft, natural colors she had applied to her face didn't look overdone, but added to her features. He figured he'd be the luckiest man at the function. He swallowed hard again.

He watched in a daze as she took the clear plastic box that contained a corsage from his shaking hand.

"You shouldn't have," she said as she took the small white rose out of the container. She cradled the delicate flower in her palm. "It's beautiful."

"May I pin it on you?"

She looked up at him with such wide eyes, he thought he had offended her.

"Are you sure you're up to it?"

"What do you mean?" he asked, utterly confused.

"Well, for a few moments, I thought something was wrong. Your knees shook, your hand trembled, and it looked as if you wanted to faint. I want to make sure you're all right, that if you come near me you won't draw blood by sticking me or fall at my feet."

"I assure you I'm fine and it would be my pleasure to assist you with it." In two steps, he closed the few feet between them and took the bloom out of her hand.

* * * *

A delightful shiver ran through her fingers at his touch. All the earlier annoyances and apprehension melted away, replaced by giddy excitement as she watched him begin the task of pinning his gift on her.

With his attention focused elsewhere, she studied him. She couldn't believe how well he cleaned up. Not that he was a bad-looking guy in dirty jeans and a t-shirt, but he was absolutely fabulous in a tuxedo. He looked the proper gentleman with his hair gelled back and no trace of stubble on his face. The black tux fit him like a glove. *It must have been tailor-made.*

The collar of his crisp white shirt was closed with a black onyx gold-rimmed button clasp, and instead of a cummerbund, he wore a silk white vest. She sighed and caught a whiff of his cologne, musky but sharp, a sensual scent. Her own knees began to shake. If only her mom could see him. She wouldn't be so quick to judge.

A sharp prick near her arm brought her attention around.

"I'm sorry." He held the flower and pin away from her. "I guess I'm trying so hard not to hurt you, yet I can't help but hurt you."

"That's all right. Here, let me." She took the pin out of his hand, and as he held the flower in place, she attached it to the wide strap of her dress right under her shoulder. There was no way to avoid touching him. Each time her fingers stroked his hand, her skin tingled.

If the mere touches made her weak in the knees now, how in the world would her body react when she danced with him later? A quiver of expectation ran through her.

"Have I told you yet how beautiful you look?"

He pulled her fingers to his mouth, kissed the back of her hand. Though his lips were but a whisper on her skin, the contact reacted as if she had been seared with a branding iron.

"No, you haven't," she replied quietly, stunned, but pleased by his words and gestures.

ตด๛ตด๛ตด๛

"Well, I should have."

His gaze locked with hers. She thought she would melt from the smoldering flames she saw in them. There was such an expression of promise, of attraction, of trust in them. The pit of her stomach churned. She didn't want to hurt him, to see those beautiful eyes look at her with the heat of hatred. But she had no choice. What if her stalker went after him? Harmed him in any way?

"Geoff, I…"

"Yes?" He still hadn't let go of her hand. He was rubbing the back of it with his thumb.

Tori let out a long sigh. She couldn't do it, not now, and she decided to stick to her original plan. No sense in ruining what was starting off as a very pleasurable evening.

"I wanted to say you look very handsome yourself. I have a feeling I'll be the envy of every woman there."

"And I of every man."

He freed her hand, stepped toward her and slid an arm around her waist. Drawing her close to him, he clasped her body against his. She gazed into his eyes, observed raw sexual desire smoldering within them, and couldn't remember ever being so besotted with need. As his one arm held firm to her waist, his other hand cupped the back of her head not allowing her any kind of escape. His mouth covered hers with a savage intensity matching the driving, fiery lust for him within her. A wave of hungry desire spiraled through her core. Her searing hunger for the man overrode everything else. Tori groped Geoff's ass and met his tongue with hers, thrust for thrust. She couldn't get enough of him and pressed the full length of her body against his. Equaling him in his passion, she threw her all into the kiss. Her heart sang with joy for the dormant sexuality of her body had been reawakened since she had met Geoff.

Geoff ended the kiss by resting his forehead against hers. His breath was hot and moist against her face. He hugged her tightly to him. "No use starting something we can't finish right away," he whispered, his breath even hotter against her ear. "How about if we each take a moment to catch our bearings and then get this charity ball over and done with?"

"Okay," she replied quietly, breathless, the fire of the primal urge still burning within her core. She broke from his embrace and made her way to the bathroom to fix her makeup and gain her composure. When she rejoined him in the living room, a luscious vibration shook her body when she looked at him.

"Now, my lady, our carriage awaits."

She picked up her cloak and purse off the chair, and rested her hand in the crook of his offered arm. They stepped out of the house.

A white stretch limousine idled in the driveway.

Her fingers dug into his elbow. "For us?" She looked up at him expectantly.

"But of course. You didn't think I'd take you to a ball in my truck, now did you?"

"Well…"

"Oh, ye of little faith. Come, let us be off."

She settled on the soft brown leather seat inside the large vehicle and stretched out her legs. Geoff got in and sat beside her. From the portable bar, he produced a small bottle of champagne and two champagne flutes.

"You didn't have to go through all this trouble," she said thickly. The responsibility of what lay ahead for her, especially with what had just transpired, welled up inside of her and threatened to gush out. She choked it back.

"It was no trouble at all," he said and handed her a glass. "Some friends of mine owed me some favors. I called them in."

Well, if he took the time to arrange all this, I can make the best of it. She could deal with her feelings of extreme guilt later.

"If I knew better, Mr. McKenzie, I'd say you're infatuated with me and trying your best to court me," she said playfully, taking a sip of the sweet liquid.

"I have only the best of intentions for you, my dear." He removed the glass from her hand and lightly kissed her on the mouth.

"Oh, Geoff." She reached up and gently brushed his cheek. *If only I could say the same.*

His lips brushed against hers twice more.

"You know you shouldn't be doing all this." She placed her hand on his smooth cheek, caught his gaze and tried to warn him with her look, to say he shouldn't continue to pursue this course of action. "For all you know, come Monday I could be a very attached and unattainable woman."

He groaned and pulled away, focusing on the passing scenery outside the window.

"I'm sorry, but it's true. I have yet to make a decision, and I don't want to hurt you in the process." She reached out and had barely touched his shoulder when he flinched and turned his gaze back on her. The pain in his eyes indicated she had already hurt him. *So much for trying to warn him off.* For the most part, she had decided she wouldn't accept David's proposal, especially with David's attitude of late and what had happened with Geoff in the park. But she couldn't tell Geoff that, not yet. All she wanted to do at the moment was to soften the blow she would later have to deal him.

"Victoria, I'm stronger than you think. Besides, the only way you could truly hurt me right now is *not* to be honest with me and so far you have been. You don't know how much I value that you can talk to me and state what's on your mind. I know what Monday may bring, but for tonight you're mine." He placed his hand on hers possessively. "And I want this night to be special. Plus, with what I felt from you in your house, I believe I don't have cause to worry."

๛๛๛๛๛๛

Conflicting emotions warred within her. Peaceful bliss that he should care so much about her, value her, want to ensure she has a pleasant evening. Anger and resentment that someone wanted to ruin her newfound happiness.

She knew she should tell him about the letters, let him help her solve the problem. But she also knew the person, or persons, behind the threats would somehow find out, and then she feared the culprits would go after him. She couldn't let any harm happen to Geoff. If anything befell him, she'd feel guiltier than she already did. And she hurt all the more because, though he believed her to be honest, she hadn't been. How was she to tell him it wasn't David who was coming between them, but some unknown abominable factor? But if he wanted tonight to be exceptional, she would relent and let him have a wonderful evening. Complying was the least she could do.

"The night will be excellent," she finally replied, squeezing his hand.

The date will be great, that is, until I tell you I can't see you anymore. But she'd worry about that later.

CHAPTER SEVENTEEN

A long banner hung from the ceiling above the escalator welcoming guests to the Twenty-first Annual St. Peter's Children's Banquet. At the top of the moving stairway outside the banquet room, a young boy and a young girl sat behind a table draped in a gold cloth. The little girl, no more than ten years old, asked them for their tickets. Victoria handed them to her. Out of the corner of her eye, she saw Geoff bend at the waist.

"My, what a pretty lady," he crooned to the girl. "That is a lovely hat and dress you're wearing. Pink suits you. I may have to fight off the men to have a dance with you."

She blushed ferociously while the boy next to her made a gagging sound.

"Oh," Geoff said with disappointment. "Seems to me you're already taken with this handsome young man here."

The boy blushed. The pink of his cheeks contrasted against his white baseball cap and black tuxedo.

"I'm not taken with nobody. Sign here." He pushed a register at them, which was knocked askew when the girl elbowed him. He gave her a quick glare. "Please."

Geoff righted the clipboard, then signed his and Victoria's names with a flourish.

"Here's your brochure," the girl said shyly. "Don't lose it. It has your silent auction number inside. Your table number is twenty. Have fun."

"Thank you," she and Geoff replied in unison as they turned toward the receiving line.

Lined up outside of the hotel's largest banquet room were
all the board members of the hospital. As she, Geoff and
others proceeded from the welcome table to the room, the
board members greeted each person with a quick *hello* and
thank you for coming. At the end of the line, two more boys in
formal wear and plain black baseball caps stood near the
doors and nodded to the guests.

The party was underway inside the large hall. Waiters and
waitresses carefully balanced their trays as they nimbly
maneuvered around the patrons at the outskirts of the dance
floor.

"Ooh, look over there," Tori exclaimed, glad she was in
attendance and had kept her mouth shut. She pointed to the
left side of the room where the items were set up for the silent
auction. "I want to spend some money. Look in the book. Is
there anything of interest being auctioned?"

"Well, let's see." Geoff opened the brochure. "A couple of
day spas have donated time to their clinics. A salon has
offered a lucky person, or should I say woman, a day of
beauty—from her head to her toes. She'll even receive free
makeup from the makeover." He slid a look at her.

She shook her head and wrinkled her nose.

"No, huh? If not that, then there's financial planning that
comes with a portfolio set-up and a year's worth of
transactions. Cleaning service for six months. Different types
of furniture." He flipped through the brochure, scanning the
pages. "Some travel agencies have packages available to
different places. There's computer related donations, books,
music, movies, dinners. Here." Geoff handed her the booklet.
"It'd be faster if you flipped through this. Right now, I'm
famished and I plan to go fill my belly at the buffet over
there." He pointed to the opposite side of the room.

"Okay. I'll meet you back at our table in a little bit."

Tori graciously accepted his peck on her cheek.

Over at the auction tables, she studied each bid sheet. There were only two to three notations on each of them except for one, which had eight and the amount was up to thirty-five hundred dollars. She leafed through the information to find the item.

"Figures the trip to the Grand Caymans would be popular," she said out loud.

She stepped back and continued to browse through the pages. More people came over to place their bids. If she played her cards right and waited a bit longer, she'd have a better chance of winning something by jotting down a bid right at the end.

The prize would have to be an item designated for two or more people since she wanted to be able to share what she won. From her purse, she procured a pen and began crossing out single person items, leaving a handful of dinners, amusement park tickets and three trips. With the choices narrowed down, she found herself faced with the question of who she'd share her win with. There was Sally—that is if Sally started to speak to her again. There was Geoff, as long as she didn't break up with him. Then, of course, there was David. She really wanted one of the trips, though, and there was no way she'd travel with David. Not anymore.

Sally or Geoff would be one of the lucky ones to accompany her to a beautiful bed and breakfast weekend in Ocean City, a Smokey Mountain winter retreat ski vacation, or fabulous Las Vegas. She sighed, remembering her predicaments with both people. If neither of them can go, she thought, I can always give the trip to my parents. A slow smile crept over her face as she made her choice.

"You look like a cat that's gotten into the cream."

"Mrs. Sims," Tori said, placing a hand over her racing heart. "You startled me."

"I'm sorry if I alarmed you, but you were a bit deep in your thoughts. Choosing an item to bid on?"

৵ঔৼঔৼঔ

"Yes. It took some time, but I finally made up my mind on one of the trips."

"That's good. Perhaps you and your fiancé will be able to get away for a little pre-honeymoon. By the way, where is your Mr. Lloyd? I'd like to offer him my congratulations as well."

Who was this woman? How the hell did she know about the proposal? Who else had David run his mouth off to? And, of course she'd be happy, she thought, wanting to wipe the smug smile off the woman's face. With her engaged, Geoff would be free for Bertha. She'd have to burst the woman's bubble. "David's not here, Mrs. Sims, and he is *not* my fiancé."

"That's interesting," she said, taking a step back. Her face took on an incredulousness expression. "Bertha's friend's cousin's brother-in-law's uncle works at the restaurant where the proposal happened. Words were spoken. A ring was presented."

"Well, your sources are wrong. The sister's aunt's bi-lingual nanny's monkey of an uncle only has a part of the story right. David asked. He produced a ring, but I did *not* accept. Therefore, we are *not* engaged." She had spoken so hastily even she didn't understand half of what she had said, and by the flabbergasted look on Gertrude's face, neither had she.

A waiter with a tray of champagne filled flutes passed by. Tori swiped one off and drank it down. Another waiter passed by and she handed him the empty glass.

"If you're not here with David, then who—"

"Ladies."

Never more grateful for an interruption than she was at that moment, she offered Geoff a shameless grin. "Hello, darling." She purred as his arm slipped around her waist. "You know Mrs. Sims, don't you dear?"

"Yes, we've had the pleasure of meeting once or twice," he replied, giving Tori a perplexed glance her way. "How are you, Mrs. Sims?"

"Quite well. Thank you for asking." Her gaze darted between the two of them. "I was under the impression, Mr. McKenzie, these types of functions weren't your cup of tea. If I had known you were going to make an appearance here, I would have brought Bertha along." She let out a long, tired sounding breath. "Too late now, I suppose. Perhaps some other time you two could get together and become better acquainted." She gathered a handful of her gauzy, pastel yellow dress and hiked it up an inch. "Be sure to say hello to Stanley before you leave, Mr. McKenzie."

"Will do, Mrs. Sims."

Once she was out of earshot, he dropped his arm from around Tori's waist and spun her to face him. "Now what was all that about, *darling?*"

"What was what all about?" she questioned in return playing the situation off as if she didn't know what he talked about.

"That." He pointed in the direction of Mrs. Sims exit. "And the *darling*, the *dear*, the batting of the eye lashes. One moment you were all claws with the woman, then you became a kitten."

"Oh, *that* what. I was attempting to diffuse a rumor. Somehow word has spread like wild fire that David and I are engaged, which you and I both know isn't true."

"Lucky for you then I came over when I did."

"Yeah, thanks. By the way, your arm around my waist was a nice touch, but I'm not sure it was a wise idea."

"It was a fine idea. You have to remember she's still out to get me for her daughter. It not only helped you, but helped my cause as well."

"I feel so used," she mocked in a hurt tone and put the back of her hand to her forehead.

"You may feel used," he said slow and deep, stepping in closer to her so he was an inch away, "but you have to admit you enjoyed it, you little minx."

ಲೆಗೊಲೆಗೊಲೆಗೊ

"You have me there," she said, then added jokingly, "You big brute of a man."

"You know what else you'd enjoy?"

Her knees trembled when the warmth of his breath caressed her ear. Her mind reeled back to the episode in her living room. *Oh boy, do I know what I'd enjoy.*

"A few turns around the dance floor with this big brute." He grasped her hand and directed her through the milling guests to the temporary hardwood square in the center of the room.

Half an hour later, exhausted, she made her way back to the table with Geoff in tow.

"Where the hell did you learn to dance like that?" She dropped into a chair, took off her shoe and rubbed her foot.

"I come from a very large and somewhat extended family where the older generation of women wanted their men to know how to dance. On top of their teachings, Sue Ellen and I took some lessons before we got married."

"Those lessons paid off."

"My aunts would be proud. I'm going back over to the buffet. Would you like anything?"

"No." She waved him off. "I'm going to check out the auction sheets once I feel the blood return to my lower extremities."

"You better hurry your circulation along. There's only fifteen minutes left for making bids and then the ceremony will start."

"Thanks for the warning." She waited till Geoff had disappeared into the crowd before she stood to test her sore feet.

"Steady as she goes," she said to no one in particular and snatched another drink off the tray of a passing waiter.

Tori was two-thirds of the way to the auction tables when her path was blocked.

"My, my, my. Who do we have here?" a low, throaty voice probed.

The hairs on her neck rose and tickled her skin. *And tonight was supposed to be enjoyable.* She gulped down her drink. "Linda, what a surprise. You never mentioned you would be here."

"Neither did you." Linda's thick, bony fingers clutched her companion's arm tightly. "Then again, it is hard to chat with co-workers when they're not at work, isn't it, Victoria?"

"Yes, it is," she replied, noticing the man's stare wasn't trained on Linda, but on her own chest. She looked down at her cleavage, then threw him a disapproving glare.

He took the hint well. He yawned and focused his attention elsewhere in the room.

Linda jerked on his arm.

"Sorry, my dear. Thought I saw someone I knew."

"Who?"

"Who what?" he asked, puzzled.

"Never mind," Linda said, as if trying to rid her mouth of a bad taste. "So, Victoria, I hear congratulations are in order?"

"Congratulations for what?" she asked, though she knew very well what the *what* was.

"Why, for your engagement, of course. You know, yours and David's. Though I do think it's wrong of a lady to consent to one man and then be seen out with another."

So the wild fire isn't contained yet. "Well, Linda, *I* think it's a faux pas to congratulate someone when you don't have your facts straight. I haven't given him an answer yet, so it should seem *obvious* to *everyone* that I am *not* engaged."

"Okay, okay." She held up her hands, palms out with a wide grin plastered on her face. "No need to get your panties in a twist."

"My panties are not in a twist," she seethed, her hatred for the woman growing. She clutched the stem of the empty glass in her fingers.

Linda's companion chose that moment to step in between them. He carefully pried Tori's fingers away from the delicate glass in her hand and took it from her.

"Henry," Linda's voice was stern, "please do not interrupt us."

"Lin," he said, turning to face her. "You don't want to cause a scene, do you? People are beginning to stare."

She cast a look around, then shook her head. She lowered her head like a child being reprimanded for a bad deed.

"Now be a good girl and go get us some drinks." He handed over the glass in his hand.

She moved to leave, but Henry paused her and whispered to her. Her ear to ear grin returned. He gave a playful swat to her tush and she giggled.

"And be quick about it," he called out as she walked away.

The tall, gangly man turned to Tori. His face, narrow and angular, looked like it could cut glass and his skin appeared ghost-like against his jet black hair. His equally dark eyes focused on hers.

"I'm Henry Whitmore, by the way." He held out his hand.

"So I gathered," Tori replied, offering hers in return.

He accepted her hand and began to rub the backs of her fingers.

"I must say, you are a very attractive woman."

She cocked an eyebrow.

"Not good at receiving compliments, are we? That's a shame. I for one don't understand why the gentleman you're with doesn't take you upstairs to one of the suites and have his way with you."

Her mouth dropped open and he leaned in toward her.

"I know I would," he said only so she could hear and the corners of his mouth twitched upward.

"Henry," Linda called out from several feet away. She made quick time back with two drinks in her hands.

"If I were you, Mr. Whitmore," Tori said quietly but succinctly, bothered by his forwardness, "I would mind my mouth and manners the rest of the evening. By the way, your date is back."

He straightened to face Linda and smiled pleasantly in response to her frown. "Hello, love." He took his drink from her.

"Don't *love* me," Linda said to him while glaring at Victoria, then added pointedly, "Isn't two enough for you?"

"I wouldn't know," Tori's voice rolled cold and steady. She didn't like Linda's implications.

"This is my cue to leave," Henry said, his focus bouncing from one woman to the other as they continued to stare each other down. "Unlike most of the male species, I don't care to see *ladies* fight with each other. When you're done with your battle, Linda, you'll find me at our table."

"Fine." Linda's stare stayed trained on Tori.

"It was a pleasure meeting you, Victoria."

"Yeah, pleasure." Her voice oozed sarcasm. She, too, didn't take her attention off her co-worker.

Tori observed Henry out of the corner of her eye as he glanced at each of them, shake his head and saunter off.

"Did Mummy and Daddy give you another silver spoon so you could come here?" Linda inquired in a cooing voice like she talked to an infant. "Or did fairy godmother, Sally, wave her magic wand in your direction again?"

"What the hell are you talking about?"

"Oh, don't play stupid with me. You know damn well what I'm talking about. I bet it was Sally who got you in here since I'm fairly sure you don't have an extra grand lying around. If you did, I'm guessing you would have put that money into repairing that dreadful little hovel you live in, and not pay for tickets at five hundred dollars a plate. But then again, you are working on your little mouse hole, aren't you? And getting the labor pretty cheap to boot. Another courtesy from *Queen Sally*.

She gives you everything, doesn't she? Whether it's direct or not, you get the good accounts, more money, extra perks. You even got David and now Geoff in the bargain. Perhaps I should take lessons from you on how to utilize my womanly wiles. Better yet, I'll give you some advice."

"I don't want any of your advice. If you don't mind—" Tori turned to leave.

"Oh, you're not going anywhere."

Linda seized her arm and dug her acrylic fingernails into her skin. Her grip was strong and Tori wondered where her co-worker got her superhuman strength.

"You're going to stay right here and hear me out," Linda's voice hardened ruthlessly. "My advice is to be careful. I've been around a lot of men like Geoff. I've seen the way he looks at you when you're paying attention to him and especially when you're not. A man like him wants only one thing, and when he gets what he wants—"

"Excuse me?" The simple question was full of shock. Tori jerked her arm out of Linda's grip.

"Get real, Victoria. The whole office knows you're the biggest prude there is. It's possibly one of the reasons David wants to marry you. So he can finally get some. Anyway, as I was saying, once Geoff gets what he wants, he'll leave you quicker than you can blink."

"That's not why David wants to marry me, and as for Geoff, you don't know him. He wouldn't. He's not like that."

"I may not know Geoff personally, but I know his type. I'll bet anything he's made some grand overtures toward you—a little wine, dining, flowers, that necklace most likely—but he hasn't said he loves you, has he?" She tilted her head as if studying a piece of art. "By the look on your face, I'm right. He's gearing up. Now all he has to do is say those three little magic words and you'll be all his."

"You're wrong." Her voice sounded choked up.

"I'm right and you know it. All men are like that. They'll do just about anything to get what they want. Kind of like you. Tell me, my little brown-nose, teacher's pet. Victoria, if we had male bosses, you'd give up your priggish manners and sleep you're way to the top, wouldn't you?"

Tori grit her teeth, clenched her fists at her sides. Her body grew hot as her blood boiled within her, pumped thickly through her arteries and veins heating every inch to a furious rage. She fought with all her strength to keep her hand from flying out to slap the coarse woman's face or choke her with the wide neck band she wore. But, she'd be damned if she stooped to Linda's level by lashing out. Instead, she took a deep cooling breath. "Thank you for your advice. I will keep what you said in mind." With her head held high, her back ramrod straight, she went to the auction tables.

One of the board members started to collect the papers. Fortunately, the item she wanted to bid on was at the opposite end of the table where he was. She hurried to the end and hastily scribbled down her number and amount on the sheet for the trip she wanted.

Seconds later, the gentleman was beside her and picked up the form. "Looks like you won," he said.

"Yes, it seems I have," she replied with confidence and then headed toward the doors.

CHAPTER EIGHTEEN

How dare Linda talk to me like that.

Spying Geoff's waiting limousine, Tori hiked up her dress and trekked across the manicured lawn. The cool night air outside of the hotel did nothing to dampen the flames of rage boiling her blood. She hadn't done anything to deserve that woman's callous remarks and her spitefulness. Her vexation grew.

She wasn't a brown-nose teacher's pet, and even in her party days, she wouldn't have slept her way to the top. She worked hard to make a name for herself and she had been lucky, being in the right places at the right times. That's why she had what she had.

And I wasn't born with a silver spoon in my mouth. Her father had worked his butt off and had invested wisely. That's why her family was what people would call *privileged*. A person's lifestyle and success wasn't handed to him or her. Achievements and prosperity had to be sought out, found and reined in.

Her pace slowed as she realized the root of Linda's hostility. The woman was jealous.

Heavy, quick-falling steps echoed behind her.

"Linda," she shouted without turning around, "I don't want to talk to you, so go away."

"Victoria. Stop. It's me."

Geoff's voice washed over her like a soothing balm. She spun to face him and in her haste crashed to the ground. Her ankle and leg twisted at an awkward angle beneath her. The contents of her purse, which popped open upon its impact with the earth, lay strewn about.

"Are you all right?" he asked, holding out his hands to assist her.

"Physically, I think so. Nothing seems to be broken…except my pride." She placed her hands in his and let him pull her up. A small cry escaped her lips. "Damn. I would have to twist the same ankle of the foot I kicked the futon with." She was grateful when he put his hands on her shoulders. His light pressure made her steadier than she felt.

"Can you stand on your own for a few moments?"

The concern in his voice, on top of all the events of the evening, brought a well of tears to her eyes. She nodded for fear that if she spoke, she would break down and sob. He crouched down and picked up the articles from her bag. Tori tried not to shift her position off her good foot.

"There. I think I've got everything." Geoff cradled the items into the crook of his left arm, and with his right, he braced her around the waist. "Now, with my support, can you hobble your way over to the car?"

She nodded again.

"Good. I'm taking you home and tending to that ankle of yours."

"I'm sorry if I ruined your evening," she said when they were safely ensconced in the vehicle.

"You have nothing to be sorry about." He put his arm around her and had her lie her head on his shoulder. "You didn't ruin my evening. I was coming over to see if you wanted to leave anyway, but I missed you. Linda informed me you weren't feeling well and that you had left. She's not a nice person, is she?"

"She's a bitch."

"I was trying to be polite."

She snuggled in closer to him, reveling in his warmth and strength.

"Geoff?"

"Yes?"

"Thank you," she whispered.

"Thank you?" he questioned back just as quietly.

"For being my friend."

With his free hand, he cupped her chin and tilted her head up.

"My dear, Tori, don't you know? Can't you tell I want to be so much more than just your friend?"

"So do…" The crinkle of paper stopped her words. Her gaze broke from his wonderful eyes shimmering in the light of the passing street lamps.

"Ah, the escapees," he joked as he plucked a few of the items left out of her purse from under his leg. "So what do we have here? Love letters, perhaps?"

"Here. Let me have them," she said, reaching for the papers in his hand. There was no way she wanted him to see them, find out about what was going on and what would happen this way.

"Hmm… How do I love thee?" he questioned, turning his body so she couldn't get the pages. "Let me count the ways," he continued, unfolding each piece.

"Geoff, I don't think—"

"Stop seeing him or else. Cease and Desist. You can't run…" He trailed off. The harsh tone of his voice hung in the air. Geoff flipped through the pages several times, the set of his face growing grimmer with each passing second.

She slid over to the other end of the seat.

"What is all this?" He positioned his body to face her. "I'm no expert, but these sound a lot like threats. Have you gone to the authorities? Does anyone else know about them?"

His hot poker stare, flashing in the passing lights, pierced her. Tori shivered, suddenly feeling weak and vulnerable. She hated those sensations.

"I don't know what they mean," she replied in a choked voice, not ready to deal with him quite yet, but now forced to. "And no, no one else knows about them. I believe someone doesn't want us to be together, but who or why…" She shrugged her shoulders. "I haven't paid them much mind. You and I are adults. We're friends. There's no harm in that, right? I guess you could call those papers threatening if you want. And to answer your other question, no, I have not gone to the police."

She watched him shake his head, his expression filled with disappointment.

"What would the authorities do or say?" she continued. "What could they do? Nothing. They would think I'm some ninny and laugh at me. Being called a hysterical female with no brains by the police, those wonderful men who are supposed to be compassionate and helpful to those in need, once in my life is good enough for me. The notes," she said distastefully, pointing to the papers in his hand, "aren't enough evidence to act upon, and the officers would only tell me what I already know. That there's nothing they can do unless something happens to me. That I should stop seeing you."

"Stop seeing me?"

"Yes. I planned to call off our relationship tonight. At first, I considered doing so on the way to the banquet, but then I changed my mind and decided to wait until after."

"Well, now it's after," he said, crumpling the notes into his fist. He leaned back against the seat with his arms folded across his stomach, his face etched with pain and his jaw taut with anger. "Fire away."

"Geoff." She reached out and touched his shoulder.

He jerked away.

Tori flinched at his curtness and lowered her hand. She had some explaining to do and fast, before the damage she had caused could no longer be repaired.

ᗷᗫᗷᗫᗷᗫ

"Look, earlier you said you valued my honesty, so now you'll listen to me." The glare he threw her way made her shudder, but she plowed ahead. "I figured I'd beg off, tell you I was swamped with work, that I had David to consider, that I needed time. I wanted to use any excuse I could so we'd stop whatever it is that's happening between us. I wanted to make you think I was the bad guy and not you."

"It sounds like you've changed your mind. Have you? *Again?*" He turned to face her, his arms still crossed over his body.

"Yes. I intended to ask that we stop seeing each other. Not because *I* wanted to, but because I felt I *had* to. I couldn't bear it if you got hurt because of me. God knows, I don't want to hurt you in any way, and it's pained me deeply to think about all this. But, if you were harmed, I know that would be worse. I only thought of your safety and keeping you from the trouble that seems to be brewing around me. But I can't. Lord, help me, I can't." She inched closer to him. "Until you, I didn't know I could feel so much again. That I could laugh and smile so much. I see now the past couple years of my life were pretty stagnant up till the day of the auction. It didn't use to be that way, but... Well, that's in the past." She reached out and laid her palm against his cheek. "Until you I didn't know I could love again."

"Does this mean you're not casting me aside?"

She nodded vigorously.

* * * *

"Victoria. My wonderful Tori." Geoff opened his arms, grabbed her to him, and held her tightly. His nose burrowed into her hair, breathing in the faint scent of her. "I care so much about you it scares me sometimes. I don't know what I'd do if you walked out of my life." He let out a long sigh, blowing wisps of her hair out of place. "I don't think I want to know. I don't think the world would, either, because I would tear it apart searching for you to get you back."

"You would do that?"

She looked up at him with such naked trust, his heart swelled with protectiveness.

"Mark my words, love. I would move heaven and earth for you."

The brilliant smile she gave in reply was all the encouragement he needed. Without further thought, he bent his head down and claimed her lips with his own. The kiss was a delicious sensation, made more wondrous when her arms wrapped around him. He could easily lose himself in her embrace. She had that power over him, even if she didn't realize it. He thanked whichever fate it was that had a hand in bringing her into his life, showing him he could love again. He pulled away, shocked at the turn his thoughts had taken.

The papers and her purse fell to the floor. He gave them a cursory glance, then focused back on her. She sat there, still holding on to him, as he was her, her eyes hooded with passion.

His mouth returned to hers, more demanding this time. Her response was eager, and she shuddered beneath his fingers. Oh, how he wanted to claim more from her than just her mouth. He wanted to explore every inch of her. He guided his hand around to the front of her body. He was less than an inch away from cupping her breast when the limo came to a stop. A disappointed sigh escaped his mouth and blew into hers. Not wanting to break contact, he outlined her jaw with a few kisses, then rested his check against hers. "I think our carriage has arrived, my lady."

"I would believe you are right, my good sir." She looked over his shoulder and out the window.

He broke himself from their embrace and got out of the car.

* * * *

Muffled voices from the front filtered through to Tori. She paid them no mind and took the few moments of privacy to pick up the scattered letters and her purse from the floor.

"Come here, girl," Geoff said, standing outside the open door on her side. "I'll carry you inside. No sense putting any unnecessary weight on that ankle till we see how bad it's damaged."

He swept her up easily into his arms. She nestled her large purse in her lap and sorted through it to find her keys. At the door, he carefully maneuvered her into his arms so she had access to the lock. After they were inside and he had kicked the door shut behind them, he took her straight to her bedroom.

"Stay here," he said, depositing her on the bed and taking her purse from her. "I'm going to find something to wrap your ankle in and get some ice."

"Yes, sir," she said with a salute.

When he returned, he looked thoroughly exasperated.

"What are we going to do with you? You have nothing in your bathroom to tend a sprain, not to mention that you're out of storage baggies." He held up a yellow plastic bag from the supermarket. "This is all I could find that would hold ice, and even then, I had to line the bottom of it with paper towels since there's a hole."

She giggled.

"I see nothing funny about this. If we don't take care of your injury, you'll have trouble putting shoes on. I don't think Sally wants you strutting around the office in bare feet."

"Baggies?" She chuckled again.

His eyebrows rose in seeming annoyance.

"I'm sorry." She couldn't help laughing. "But to hear a big strong man like you say *baggies* struck me funny."

"Tori…" He drew out her name, the tone of his voice a warning.

"Okay. Okay." She pointed to her dresser. "There's an old cream-colored slip in the back of the top drawer. You can use that to wrap my ankle."

* * * *

Geoff turned with a huff. She was infuriating, yet so refreshing. He pushed aside those thoughts as he neared the drawers, remembering one night after Sue Ellen had run off, when he, Phillip and a few other guys had broken into a sorority house. Phil and his friends had been rushing at fraternity at their college and one of their tasks had been to plan and successfully complete a panty raid on the frat's sister house.

Because he had attended night school, he had missed out on the finer aspects of college and thought that by joining his cousin and Phil's cohorts, the escapade would make up for it. Plus, there was a woman Phil had introduced him to whom he had been interested in and she had lived there. He thought he'd surprise her.

The panty heist had gone off without a hitch, yet he had never seen the pretty sophomore. After he and all the other guys had claimed their souvenirs from their chosen girls' rooms, they had returned to the frat house to find they had been pranked as well. The trees out front had been littered with toilet paper, shaving cream and the fraternity members' underwear. Across the street, the sisters and their housemother had laughed, then had gone on their merry way singing their chapter's song.

I hope I'm not being had right now, he thought. It had been a bit of time since he last had sex. Seeing Tori lie there on the bed had raised more than just memories of boyish shenanigans.

He took a deep breath and pulled open the drawer. The task should be simple enough, he told himself. After all, she did say it was in the back. His hands slipped in and guided their way through cotton, lace, and silk. He pushed aside some bras and panties, so sheer they were almost transparent. When they touched upon a soft garment, he pulled it out believing he had found what he was looking for.

The garment unraveled to reveal itself as a slinky red teddy with so little fabric the piece would leave nothing to the imagination. And, if she had a piece like that in her drawer, God only knew what she wore under her dress. With a groan, he tossed it back in and adjusted the fabric of his pants at his groin. On his next attempt, he pulled out the correct slip.

"I have to tear this up," he said, not turning around for fear he wouldn't be the only one embarrassed by the erection he possessed.

"That's fine," her soft voice said from behind. "At least, it will be put to good use one last time."

With each tear of the cloth, the throbbing in his groin subsided. Once his arousal was under control, he brought the strips of cloth over to her.

She sat holding the ice pack on her ankle.

"It might work better if you took your hose off, you know."

"Yeah, I guess you're right."

She brought her legs together, her knees bent toward him. He sucked in his breath. She shifted and wiggled, her dress bunching up her hips with each movement. His gaze continued to linger on her legs as she slipped the silky material down her thighs and over her calves, revealing their creamy white smoothness. If someone had told him that watching a woman relieve herself of her panty hose could be erotic, he never would have believed it. But obviously, seeing was believing, and he was mesmerized.

"Mr. McKenzie, I do believe it's impolite to stare."

He blinked several times, and within those moments, she had straightened out not only her legs but her dress as well. His attention snapped to her face. She grinned mischievously and her eyes sparkled with merriment.

"Did you enjoy the show?" Her words floated out in a lazy, seductive drawl.

"Wha…?" All his brain function ceased.

"Do you wish you had some dollar bills to toss my way?"

"Yes." He shook his head. "I mean no," he added and spun away from her tempting sight. He couldn't let her bewitch him. "It might be best for you and the sake of your dress if you changed into more comfortable clothes. Let's say," he paused and thought of an outfit that would turn a man's desire cold, "an oversized sweat shirt and sweat pants?" Without waiting for an answer, he strode purposefully to her dressers.

He slid a heated moist palm over his face. Hell, he wanted to wrap her in so many layers of clothes she'd be ready for the Arctic Circle. It was either that or nothing at all, and he doubted she'd like the second option.

"Sounds good to me," she replied with a soft chuckle. "Third drawer down you should find what you need."

He shuffled through her belongings once again and upon finding the biggest, heaviest pieces he could, he pitched them to her with barely a glance in her direction.

She had the gall to laugh at him. *Again*. He leaned against the dresser and threw her a disgruntled look, hoping she'd see he wasn't happy being mocked.

"Oh, Geoff, I'm sorry for my teasing. But you should have seen how you looked at me—like a hungry wolf after a prize sheep." When he didn't reply, she let out a long sigh. "So, Mr. Wolf, if you don't want to see this ewe shed her wool, you should leave the room."

"I think that's the most sensible suggestion you've made all evening," he said, heading for the door.

"Could you do me a favor while I change? Could you put those damn letters in an envelope for me? You'll find large ones in my desk. Then mark it for the police so I don't confuse it with anything else."

"Sensible decision number two." He looked over at her. "I'm glad you're finally going to get the authorities involved."

"Yeah, well, it's about time I do a lot of things. Now, scoot, or else I'll never get the wrinkles out of this outfit."

Putting the letters in a larger envelope took less than three minutes. As the proceeding minutes ticked by, he paced around the living room, checked with the limo driver to make sure he was all right and didn't mind waiting a while longer. Then he deposited his tuxedo jacket, vest and collar clasp onto the couch. He paced some more and figured he'd have a well-worn grove in her floors at the rate it took for her to change. During one of the passes through the living room, he noted the time elapsed had hit ten minutes.

He didn't want to wait any longer. Tori was supposed to be getting ready for bed, not a night out on the town. Geoff had taken one step into her office when she called his name. Summoning every ounce of patience he had, he made his way back into her room.

The sight that greeted Geoff stunned him. All the lights had been turned off, save one, which was dimmed by a piece of red cloth draped over the shade. The curtains had been pulled back to let in the glow of the moon. Everything was swathed in a silvery-pinkish sheen. Even Tori. Her hair and skin were radiant, her eyes sparkling.

The moonlight enhanced her features and alerted him to the fact she hadn't put on the sweat suit. The outfit, along with the dress, was nowhere in sight. All that remained on her was a slip and the comforter wrapped around her mid-section and uninjured leg. One of the thin, silky straps of the undergarment fell to the middle of her bicep. She didn't move to correct it. She couldn't have looked sexier if she were bare.

He took in a shuddering breath. There was the faint scent of sandalwood in the air.

"Tori," his voice vibrated deeply with desire.

"You wanted to look at my ankle, right?" She held up her bare leg and wiggled her toes in the air. "How did you expect to do it properly if you made me dress like Nanook of the North?"

His mouth opened and closed wordlessly.

"Come and sit down." She patted the bed.

As he made a seat at her feet, she shifted her position. He caught an eyeful of cleavage and hastily picked up her foot.

She let out a small gasp.

"Did I hurt you?"

"Not really. It's a little tender. That's all."

It took all his strength to pull his gaze off her beautiful face. He forced his focus on her foot. From what he could see and feel, there was no swelling. The lack of bruising was a good sign, too. Using his thumbs, he began to rub the sides of her ankle.

"Does this bother you?" *Because touching you and not being able to have you is surely bothering me.*

"No. It feels quite nice," she purred.

He increased his strokes to include the sides of her foot, then the base, chanting to himself this was to help her, not turn him on.

The bed shifted.

He cast a guarded look in her direction. She had inclined against her pillows with her arms behind her head. Her eyes were closed. Her breasts swelled against the thin fabric of the slip and appeared ready to fall out of their confines. She looked quite content.

The opposite of what he felt.

"Don't stop." Her command came out a sigh.

"I don't think I can continue." He gently lowered her foot.

"Are you okay?" Her eyelids flew open and her deep blue stare bore in on him. "You look a bit flushed. You didn't eat something bad, did you?"

"I'm fine." He held up a hand to ward off her concern, then let it fall heavily into his lap. "I lied. I'm not fine. I think I should go."

"Why?" She grabbed hold of his hand to stay him.

"Why? You have to ask me why?" Damn, even to his ears he sounded angry. He closed his eyes so he wouldn't have to see her hurt expression.

"Geoff?"

There was innocence and pleading in her voice. He never thought his name could hold so much emotion. Yet, how could he explain to her he wanted to take her, taste her, feel all of her against him, and make her a part of him, without sounding crass? For all her intelligence and aside from some of their make out sessions, she still seemed so pure. Anything he said now could ruin the tenuous bond they had.

"Geoff?"

He let out a long, audible breath, pulled his hand from hers and opened his eyes. Words failed him, and since he couldn't express himself verbally, hopefully his body language would tell the tale. He pinned his gaze to hers and through it attempted to show her all his longing, passion and need. He raked his gaze methodically from her head to her chest and back again. Upon ending his assessment, it came as no surprise to see her rate of breathing had increased and there was a nice rosy flush to her face.

"Tori, I find you too attractive for my own good. Just seeing you like this… You don't know…"

"I do know," she said softly.

"No. You seem so wholesome and untainted. What I want to do with you…" He sighed and shook his head, adjusted the comforter, covering any bare parts of her he could.

* * * *

"I wouldn't worry about covering me anymore," Tori said. She stopped his hands from fidgeting with the blanket. "Let me share a little secret with you. I'm not the prude everyone believes me to be. Only Sally knows the full extent of my wild days. Am I a virgin? Far from it. Oh, so far from it. So don't think you have to be hesitant with what you want to say or do."

Geoff gazed into her eyes. "What I want is something more, something deeper. I want you to be mine. I want to us to combine with each other not as two people but as two spirits becoming a whole. No one, not even Sue Ellen, has ever affected me the way you do. What I want is to make love to you…*with* you." He removed his hand from her chin and slid it to support the back of her head.

The warmth of his palm and his surprising, heartfelt declaration sent shudders down her spine and arms.

He placed a quick kiss to her brow then on her lips.

"Just give me the word and I'll be all yours," he whispered, his breath caressing her cheek. "But, also, keep in mind it's been quite some time since…well, since I've been close to someone. From what I've heard, though, it's like riding a bike. Once you've learned…"

Tori pressed herself up against him and took his lips in a silent, demanding need. The passion she had buried long ago and deep within her exploded with the force of a geyser. She pushed and pinned Geoff down on the bed. As she spread out on top of him, his massive, solid body didn't budge under her weight. The heat already generating between them was intense. She thought she would melt from the sexual tension, from his hot skin. Yet, she couldn't seem to get near enough to him. She splayed her fingers across his shoulders and trailed a path up the side of his neck to cup his face in her hands. She forced his mouth open with her tongue, pulled his into her mouth and sucked on it, giving it a playful nip before she let it go. He kneaded her rear and the harder he grabbed, the deeper she kissed him.

Her hands worked the buttons on his shirt, and as they did, he bunched up her slip and glided his fingers under her panties. A sensuous moan escaped her mouth.

Geoff broke the kiss, rubbed his cheek against hers. "Let me make you forget all the men who came before me."

She wanted, needed, to have their bare skin touch, to achieve the closeness she craved. She stood and within seconds was nude in front of him.

"Are those tattoos?" he asked, taking off his dress shirt and undershirt. He propped himself up on his elbows.

"Yeah. Told you I had a past. I have a sun here on my left hip, a moon on my right and the stars here on my front," she answered, pointing them out and then turned presenting him with her naked ass. "And here on my back I have three more stars. They're just low enough to be covered by a decent bikini bottom." She knelt down and took off his shoes, tossing one shoe and sock aside, then the next. She climbed up onto the bed, sitting next to him, reached out, took his hand and brought it up to her face. With slow precision, she placed a kiss on each of his fingertips then turned his hand over and kissed his palm. Holding his hand tight in hers, she looked up and waited for him to look at her again. When he did, her breath caught in her throat. No man had ever looked at her with such ardor as he was at that moment. It made what she was about to say all the more easy.

"Geoff, I'm giving you the word. I don't care what anyone else has to say, or think, or do about what's between the two of us. I want you to be all mine. I want to be all yours. *Please*, make love to me."

He made no move. For several heartbeats, silence permeated the room. Had he had changed his mind about her and decided to leave anyway? She dropped his hand and looked away. Mercifully, the wan lighting in the room hid the extent of her embarrassment. She hated feeling like a fool, and the longer the silence continued, the more she felt like one.

Outside there was a rumble in the distance and, as it grew louder, the familiar vibration and hum of the motorcycle consumed her mind. For a disconcerting moment it sounded as if the rider had stopped right out front of her home. Seconds later the bike took off with a squeal and headed out into the distance.

The bed bowed next to her, and she was pulled into the warmth of Geoff's arms.

"Are you all right, Tori? You seemed to freeze there for a moment."

She took a deep breath. There was no way she was going to let her anxieties get the better of her. Not when she had a fine hunk of a man in her bed. "Yes. I'm absolutely great." Tori turned and straddled his lap. "So, how about you? Any tats?"

"Nope. No tattoos."

Before she could form another question, she was pinned down on the bed beneath his massive body and his mouth swooped down to capture hers. Tori splayed her fingers across his back and trailed a path down his sides and around to the front. The work of getting his shirt unbuttoned was slow going since their bodies were pressed together and his ardent kissing was robbing her of concentration.

Geoff sat up and made quick work of ridding himself of the piece of clothing. Placing a hand on either side of her, he leaned over her body, placed a kiss on her forehead, then whispered in her ear. "Touch away."

She gazed at him, positioned her hands on his shoulders, then slid them down feeling the all the contours and nuances of his upper torso. She brushed over his nipples and he sucked in his breath. The skin beneath her fingers was hairless, hot, and smooth. She continued to trace a path down to his abdomen, her fingernails dipping into the creases of his muscles. The area she touched tensed, shuddered, and released. When she reached the waistband of his pants, she stopped, flattened her hands on his torso and retraced her tracks back up his chest. Her thumbs brushed his nipples again. He quivered under her hands. She caressed the tiny nubs once more.

"Do you like that?" she asked seductively, pleased he was responding so nicely to her advances. She gazed into his eyes.

"Yes," he replied breathlessly.

Feeling a little more daring, she pinched the hard peaks.

"Oh, God, Tori. You're killing me. And I don't want this to be over before it gets started."

Embolden by his words, she cupped her hands over his breasts and gave them a squeeze.

He growled.

Her excitement mounted with each pleasurable sound he made. She rubbed an outward trail to his sides and skimmed downward. He was so solid and warm. The subtle scent of his aftershave and manly musk was intoxicating. Repositioning herself and him to where he was sprawled on the bed and she straddled him, she ran her tongue down the valley of his chest, then slid his pants and underwear off in one swoop and took a moment to take in the view.

"My, aren't we magnificent?" she commented, looking at his thick shaft bobbing freely in the air.

"Why, thank you. I do my best. You're not too shabby yourself."

She pulled her hair out its bun, shook the locks free and her face creased into devilish smile.

"Tori."

"Yes, dear?" she asked in a nonchalant tone in reply to the thin warning tenor of his voice. Her tongue trailed a moist line to the hairline of his navel.

"I don't..." He panted.

"Don't what?" She spread her palm against him and extended her hand down. When her fingers hit their mark, she grasped his hard shaft. His hips thrust toward her, and she increased her attentions. With Geoff, it seemed like the first time she was touching a man. Her excitement grew with each pleasurable sound emanating from him. He was so solid and warm. The subtle scent of his aftershave and heat was intoxicating.

Geoff grabbed her wrist and pulled her hand away.

"What'd you do that for? Didn't you like it?"

"I liked it just fine, but I think it's your turn now."

In mere seconds, he had her flipped onto her back, his naked body stretched on top of hers with a thigh between her legs.

Here was the nearness she had been craving, the contact of their heated skin against each other, along with the full extent of his arousal pressing against her.

"Now, my dear, it's payback time."

A river of anticipation flooded through her being and warmed her soul.

He traced every outline, every curve of her body with his hands, lips and tongue until she believed he would know it better than she. Folds of her bedspread bunched in her hands. She arched toward him when he fastened his lips around the top of a breast. He drew on the area, teasing the nipple with flicks of his tongue. While he suckled, his fingers probed the junction between her thighs, thumb and forefinger stroking her. she thought she'd expire from the sweet agony he was putting her body through. She thought she'd expire from the sweet agony he put her body through. He released her.

Sitting back, he placed his hands on her knees and opened her legs. Her hips hitched, and a moment later, Geoff's mouth fastened onto her. His hands smoothed up her thighs and held onto her hips as he stoked the fire burning within her.

Tori's fingers entwined in his silky hair. Her pulse quickened, beating in fast response to the erotic sensations stirring in her body. She moaned and writhed, but he held fast to her hips and continued to pleasure her. Her body tensed, and she cried out as a spasm of warm ecstasy vibrated through her.

He kissed his way back up her body, ending with a peck of his lips on her nose. Laying part on her, part on the bed, his knee sat between her thighs. His shaft, ready and willing, rested on the side of her lower abdomen. Nuzzling his face near her ear, he whispered, "Tell me, Victoria," his voice was heavy and thick with passion. "Tell me you want me."

"I want you." She turned her face toward his and kissed him. "Very much. There's protection in my nightstand." Tori tilted her head in its direction.

In a few swift moves, he found what he needed and prepped himself.

His gaze bore into hers. In it, she caught the fire of passion, of need, of hope. She didn't think that anymore words were needed but wanted to assure him. "Take me, Geoff. I'm yours."

Geoff pinned her to the bed under his hard body. She wrapped her arms around him, clawing her fingers along his back as throbbing desire for him to be within her strummed her senses. Tori wrapped her legs around him and her heated core enveloped him. He thrust in. A hot fire flared in her loins. She rocked beneath him in a heated frenzy, milking him for all he was worth. Sweat slicked her down as she panted and gasped in escalating bliss. Unintelligible words spewed from her and pleasurable waves of sexual satisfaction surged through her. Perspiration soaked tendrils of hair stuck to the sides of her face, but she didn't care. Another spasm rocked her body. She gripped his back until her throes of ecstasy subsided and all that was left was the light pulsing of her body surrounding his.

He trembled against her, his own release following suit. He went rigid beneath her hands, jerked his head back with a low growl, then fell upon her in a relaxed heap. She kissed his shoulder. A warm contented feeling stole over her. She was glad he had found out about the letters and that she didn't let him go.

Moments later, he eased out of her, rolled onto his back and brought her with him. She snuggled up close and sighed.

"You're mine now," he said with a tone of fierce protectiveness.

At ease and tired, she mumbled an acknowledgement and promptly fell into a satiated sleep.

* * * *

After an hour had passed, Geoff reluctantly loosened her hold on him, slid out of the bed and covered her with the comforter. As quietly as he could, he dressed.

Taking one last look at her before he left the room, he sighed. He didn't want to leave her, but he had to. In the morning after he arrived at work, he would call her, assure her of his feelings and invite her over for dinner. Perhaps if he asked nicely, she would wear the red negligee hiding in her drawer.

But stay overnight and be around in the morning, he couldn't. Though it was Saturday, he had to be at the office early, and he had some serious thinking to do.

CHAPTER NINETEEN

*T*ori brought her car to a screeching halt in Sally's driveway and stole a glance in the rearview mirror. Rigid lines creased her face. She glared back at her reflection. The scenic ride over, normally pleasant and calming, hadn't helped her mood one whit. But what had she expected? That a handful of minutes would change the *lovely* start of her day?

She should have been home making breakfast for her guy. She and Geoff should have been discussing what the future held for the two of them. But, no. Instead, the phone woke her up, and she found she was alone in her bed. Then during the call she had to listen to her friend's frantic ramblings about something horrible that had happened, but not what.

And to top it all off, Linda's voice and her oh-so-friendly advice kept clamoring for attention in her mind. *That woman couldn't have been right. Geoff hadn't used her, had he?*

She shook her head to rid herself of the thoughts. Sally and whatever her problem was that she couldn't state over the phone, needed to be her main concern. She'd hunt down Geoff for his excuses as to why he wasn't in her bed later.

Inside, Sally sat at the kitchen table sobbing into a handful of tissues. The remains of tear-soaked others lay on the floor and the table around her.

"Sally, I'm here." Tori's anger immediately dissipated upon viewing the sad scene. She hurried to her friend and knelt beside her. "What's going on? Did something happen to Frank?"

"No. Frank's out back," she hitched. She snatched more tissues from her dwindling supply and mopped her red, swollen eyes. "He's out back trying to find Snowpea."

"Find? What do you mean find Snowpea?"

"I let the dog out earlier this morning. Frank was around, so was Buck. You know we've always let Snowpea run around on his own. He liked to stretch his little legs and chase the squirrels." Her breath snagged. "I was busy in here helping Ginny clean. Frank came in. Said he had some errands to run. Shortly after, Buck let me know he was on his way. I don't remember how much time passed between their leaving and my calling for Snowpea to come in. Everything seems muddled up here." She tapped her head.

"It's okay. You don't have to give me a minute by minute replay. What happened next?" Coaxing the whole story from her friend took Tori awhile, but she learned that, after a few attempts to call in the dog, Sally had figured he had gotten into some mischief and would return in due time. It wasn't the first time he had wandered off seeking new territory so she resumed cleaning. Frank had come back, asked where the pooch was and went to look for him. That's when he found the note tacked to a tree. Her husband had run back into the house, spitting mad and barking orders. When she had gotten him to calm down a notch, he had told her what he'd found.

"At first, my shock was from the blunt way he told me my angel was gone, but once the words lodged in my mind, I became the blubbering mess you see before you now," Sally said. Tears continued to streak down her cheeks. "Frank blames Buck for this. I told him it was pure nonsense. That boy spoiled the dog as badly as we did. He never treated Snowpea with anything but affection. Frank says he's the one and only suspect and wants me to call the police." Sally shook her head as if denying her husband again.

"You weren't too shaken to call me. Even though you're none too happy with me right now due to the issues at work,"

Tori stated, a bit confused why her friend wasn't getting some type of authority involved in the dog-napping.

"Yes, well." Sally rose from the table, went to the counter, and when she returned, handed Tori a slip of paper. "I wanted to get your opinion first."

Tori scanned the familiar typeset. Shocked, blood escaped her face.

"Frank found it with Snowpea's tags. What's it all about? What does this sicko mean? 'Your dog's been taken. You shouldn't rush to give to those unworthy. Ask your friend. She'll know.' So, I'm asking. Why is my dog gone?" The last question boomed and echoed in the room.

"This is all my fault." Tori wished the floor would open and swallow her whole. She couldn't look at Sally, couldn't bear to see the woman's pain and frustration. She took a seat at the table and sighed. "I should have gone to the police long before this."

"You? How is this your fault? Why would you have to go to the police? What aren't you telling me?"

"Sit down, Sally. I have a story to tell you. Maybe then you'll understand." Once Sally took a seat across from her, she told her boss everything. She left out not one single detail, except for the full facts of her and Geoff's late night tryst. "I'm so sorry. If only I had gone to the authorities. I should have. This whole mess could have been avoided. Your poor innocent dog." A sob caught in her throat.

"Should've, could've, would've. Can't change what's been done. Here, take the last few tissues and dry your eyes. My, aren't we a pair today? I don't know about you, but I feel as if I've run an emotional gauntlet. So what should we do about this situation?"

"We?" Tori asked between sniffles.

"Yes. We. I'm involved now, too aren't I? So is Geoff. Between the three of us and with the help of our boys in blue, the culprit will be caught. Once Frank finishes checking the grounds to make sure the dog is really gone, we'll go to the station."

"But I don't have the evidence with me." She smacked her forehead. It was the first time in days she had left the house and didn't have the letters with her. "I'll have to run home and get them. I'll stop by Geoff's, and if he's home, I'll pick him up and meet you at the station across from the mall." She rose to leave.

"We'll meet you there in an hour," Sally responded.

Tori gave a nod and left.

The sun, in its usual New Jersey fall fashion, hibernated behind a blanket of gray. Tori flipped through the radio stations in her car for a weather report as she rounded Geoff's block for the fourth time. She didn't think it would rain soon, but she had hoped to find a parking spot faster than this. At this rate, by the time she parked and got Geoff, she wouldn't have enough time to get to her place, grab what she needed and meet Sally before the hour was up.

"Storms are heading in from the Northwest and aren't expected to hit our listening area till mid-Tuesday morning. Until then, temperatures will be in the mid to upper sixties under mostly cloudy skies. After the front moves through, expect temperatures to be in the low fifties. Now on to traffic. Jane…"

She turned off the radio. A car pulled out of a spot directly across from Geoff's residence. She threw on her blinker. Parallel parking had never been her strong suit, and after several attempts, she finally settled her car in between the two other vehicles and killed her engine.

A long line of traffic built up from waiting for her to park moved past and barred the view to Geoff's house across the road. Drivers and occupants glared their impatience at her as they drove by. Some were even kind enough to wave with their middle finger pointing in the air. She returned their one finger salute with one of her own thinking it would have been much easier to park if Geoff's truck hadn't taken up his whole driveway. Or if the extremely long Cadillac directly in front hadn't used more than one spot.

She turned her attention away for a moment to grab her keys and purse. When she turned back, she watched Mrs. Sims and Bertha, followed by Geoff, emerge from the house onto the porch.

So that's why he wasn't in my bed or house this morning. He had a meeting with the witches.

Tori hesitated opening her door. The women appeared very happy. Mrs. Sims grabbed Geoff's hand, pumped his arm up and down, and her mouth moved a mile a minute. Bertha stood to the other side with her head down, a sappy smile on her face, and used the toe of her shoe to scuff the wood planks.

The girl looked all too radiant for Tori's piece of mind. But it wasn't the actions of the women that amazed her and made her blink in bafflement.

It was his. He had claimed he couldn't stand them, yet there he was grinning like the Cheshire cat.

Boy, does he have a lot of explaining to do. Her right hand white-knuckled the steering wheel in her irritation.

What seemed like an eternity passed as she sat in her car waiting for the women to take their leave and for Geoff to go back inside. She remained with her hand on the door handle until the Cadillac pulled away. She had put one foot out of her car when another luxury vehicle sped into the slot the Simses had vacated.

A woman, whose beauty rivaled top fashion models, sprang from the metallic blue Sportster and bounded up the steps. Her long blonde hair flew out behind her. She had a body most women would give their souls for, not an ounce of fat, and long legs.

Tori stood, then pressed against and moved down the length of her car, wanting a clear shot of Geoff's reaction when he opened his door.

She wished she hadn't.

The complete surprise on his face turned into intense pleasure—an expression she remembered quite well from the night before. The earth-shattering grin was back, too.

She could have handled all that in and of itself, but when he swept the woman into his arms, her soul collapsed.

Distraught, she glanced at her watch and realized she only had a few more minutes until Sally expected her at the station. There was no time left. No time to tell Geoff what had happened at Sally's. No time to confront him about his revolving door for women.

Tori got back in her car, pulled out her cell phone from her purse and called Geoff as she left. Just as she had expected, and had hoped, his voice mail answered.

"Geoff. Tori. I was out front and saw you had company. We need to talk," she gritted out. "I won't disturb you right now, but I wanted to let you know Sally and I are going to the police. I'm supposed to meet her at the station right off Routes 202 and 206 in about twenty minutes. Meet us there if you can."

She disconnected the call and drove home thinking how, after she and Sally wrapped up their business at the station, she'd go to David's. It was time to formally end it with him and put her life back in order.

Leaving her car to idle in the driveway, she hurried to her house.

The sight of a white envelope taped to the door made her screech to a halt.

Why? her mind screamed.

Shaking with anger, she stormed up to the door, ripped down the newest threat and tore the envelope open.

YOU LOUSY WHORE…

ॐ∽ॐ∽ॐ∽ॐ

That was as much as she read. There was no need to finish. Her frustration would only compound, and to deal with the authorities—and later the men in her life—she needed a clear head.

Inside, she went straight to her office and retrieved the package she came for. After adding the latest arrival, she shoved the large envelope into her big purse and tried to zipper the bag. The sack wouldn't close. The thin shred of patience she had remaining snapped. With no time left to transfer the contents to her briefcase, she left the zipper undone and clutched the bulging accessory under her arm.

As she marched outside to her car, she tilted her head back and noticed the sun shone again. *What gall it has coming out to brighten everything when my day's so bleak no amount of sunshine would do any good.* She stopped anyway and kept her face lifted up to the sky to feel the warmth of the rays for a few seconds.

In an instant, her head felt like it had exploded. The stolen moment was snatched away from her in a blast of pain. Horrified, her eyelids flew open, and she was no longer looking at the sky but at the ground.

The earth rushed up to meet her and greeted her with darkness.

* * * *

"Please, come in," Geoff offered to his ex-wife once he had released her from the embrace. "I must say this is quite a surprise."

"You're telling me," Sue Ellen replied, brushing past him, and stepped into the foyer. "I wasn't expecting such a warm welcome. Especially after all these years. I thought I'd have to beg you to let me in."

"Well, don't think you're getting off *that* easy." He led her to the kitchen. "You have a lot of explaining to do, starting with why you deserted me. As for my enthusiastic greeting, don't take it to heart. A couple of ladies had just left as you arrived, and I happened to notice they had stopped and were watching us. I hugged you to put some bees in their bonnets."

"Oh. And if you hadn't been in their sights?"

"We'd be on the porch, outside still, and you'd be enlightening me there. But, since you're lucky and made it inside, have a seat. Drink?"

"Water will be fine." She sat at the table crossing her long legs.

He prepared two glasses and joined her.

She took a few sips while glancing around.

"Well?" he inquired tersely, unhappy to have the glitch of her appearance thrown into his day. He was supposed to have been at work a couple of hours ago, supposed to have called Tori, but the unexpected and unwanted visitors kept interrupting his plans.

"You've done a lot with this place. Looks like you're doing well for yourself."

"I can't complain." He sat back so he would stop getting whiffs of her overly heady flower perfume. "You don't look like you're in the poor house either. But I hope you didn't come by just to catch up on old times or to look for some kind of settlement because, if that's the case, I'll have to ask you to leave. Getting over you, Sue Ellen, took me some time and occasionally the hole in my heart your departure created still hurts. But, I've met a wonderful woman and that hole is being filled and healed. So, I'd appreciate it if you'd state your business, so I can get on with mine."

"God, this isn't going to be easy to say," she stated, clutching the glass in her hands so tightly her knuckles paled. "Guess I need to just come right out with it."

He nodded her on.

"Our son is missing."

"Excuse me?" His stomach contracted and his throat closed. The breath whooshed from his body as if he'd been punched. Geoff sat and stared at his ex-wife, a sharp pain pulsing in his forehead above his right eye. Had she gone off her rocker? They never had a kid together. "Son?"

"Our son. Yours and mine. He's missing. I've looked everywhere and had no one else to turn to. The police said not enough time has passed to be able to file a report. The school's security only deals with the campus and housing. Their cameras and tapes caught him leaving the grounds so now he's out of their jurisdiction. I've called friends. Nelson has no idea where he got off to."

"I thought," she continued, "that perhaps Zach finally found his way here. He knows Nelson isn't his biological father and even though I've told Zach time and time again that *I* left *you*, he still feels you've done me some kind of wrong. He's gone to treatment. The prep school's on-site counselor has been helpful to an extent. But still... I've feared that until he got his anger under control he may come to meet you for a confrontation."

Geoff sat back, continuing to stare at the woman. *Zach. Nelson. Prep-school. Psychologists.* Years had passed. All this had happened... He'd had a son and had no clue. No idea a part of him was out there in the world, raised by people he didn't know. He took a few deep breaths, counted to ten several times, then leaned on the table toward her.

"I have a son and you're only telling me now?" he asked in a low grumble, upset his day had gone from bad to worse.

"Actually, I never planned on telling you." She couldn't meet his stare.

"Never planned on telling me?" he bellowed, springing from the chair and slamming his hands on the table. "How could you? What in God's name is in that mind of yours? You knew I wanted kids, a family. Why did you think I was busting my ass to go to school and create a business?"

"That's exactly why," she hollered back, rising from her spot and flailing a hand in the air. "You were never here. I wanted a family, too, but I wanted to raise children *with* someone, not by myself. When I found out I was pregnant, it took me a couple of weeks to think about our situation and what I was going to do. You were in school. You were starting a business. You were rarely home. Then I figured when you were done with school you wouldn't be devoting that time to me or a family, your days and nights would be devoted to your company. And, once the business was built to your satisfaction, which it probably still isn't and probably never will be, then you'd want to play family man. Well, it'd be too late by then. I decided if I was going to be alone raising a child, I may as well *be* on my own. So I left."

"Well, that explains it, then," he said with a hint of sarcasm and retook his seat. "Why didn't you come and talk to me? What happened to our promise to be in love with each other forever? Who is this Nelson character, anyway?"

"Being in love forever. Yeah, right." Sue Ellen chortled. "We were kids. What did we know? It wasn't like I was all that much in love with you at that point. I didn't know you anymore, and you didn't seem to want to learn about the woman I was becoming. We were twenty years old. I had a life I realized I wanted. I wanted to travel, be a model, maybe act in some plays. I grew out of our relationship. We most likely would have ended up leaving each other as it was.

"Nelson's a photographer. He had a contract with the children's charity to do their photo spreads and banquet pictures. We had become friends. He did my portfolio for free. When I left you, I went to Europe with him. I modeled for women's magazines and later maternity clothing lines. We've lived together on and off for years. He's been good to me and Zachary. He's helped pay for Zach's schooling and board. Right now he's shooting in Paris. I was called away from my gig in the city by the school because of Zach's disappearance."

Sue Ellen stepped over to him and placed a hand on his shoulder. "I'm sorry you had to find out this way and if I've caused you pain. If I could have spared you this hurt, I would have. But I thought my baby was here. I thought he'd found you." She choked back a sob. "And, now he isn't. And I don't know what else to do, but I'm sure I'll think of something." Sue Ellen let go of him, opened her purse and pulled out a small white card. She handed it to him. "That has my cell phone number. I also wrote the name of the hotel I'm staying at on the back. Should an angry teen who has my eyes, your hair and nose show up, please give me a call."

She turned and made to leave, but he stopped her. "Whose last name does he have?"

"Mine," she replied with sad eyes. "I thought it would be better that way."

"Zachary Mills," Geoff said cheerlessly and showed her to the front door.

"Zachary Liam Mills. I gave him your middle name."

"Yeah? How nice of you." He opened the door for her, suddenly drained from the shock of adrenaline leaving his system. "Look, Sue Ellen, this is a lot to take in. If he happens to show up or if I happen to think of anything that might help you out, I'll let you know. For the time being, though, I'd like to be alone and give my girlfriend a call. Good-day."

At his desk in his home office, he tried to read some documents. The words on the papers blurred before his eyes. Exhausted mentally and physically from the day's events, he couldn't wrap his mind around the fact he had a son. A son he didn't know, and at this rate, if he wasn't found, he'd never know.

Sue Ellen was beside herself. Even though he had told her he'd call her if anything came up and that he wanted to be alone, it didn't matter. She kept calling him. At times she was hysterical, at others there was an icy coolness to her when she mentioned the police couldn't tell her anything. Zach's friends hadn't heard from him, the kid hadn't shown up for classes.

He looked at his clock. It was close to her hourly call, and he still had nothing to tell her.

And, speaking of disappearing people, where the hell was Tori?

After he had retrieved his messages, he had phoned her house and cell phone. He had tried Sally's lines. He had even called the station to see if the women were there. The police couldn't give out that information. He tried Tori's numbers again. Still no answers. He hung up without leaving another message considering he had already left several on each line. He tried Sally's phones, too. No luck.

After shuffling the papers he'd been viewing into a pile, he moved them to the corner of his desk. What made him think it'd be wise to try to work? He leaned back in his chair and stared out the window. He had to clear his mind and get to the tasks at hand because, after all, like Sue Ellen had said in one of her frantic phone calls, he was a workaholic. One who couldn't seem to keep a woman in his life.

CHAPTER TWENTY

Journal entry #49

Ah, my wonderful assistants have done their jobs well and soon that bitch will not be a problem anymore. Soon my loyal servant and friend will compromise her. Then he will no longer want her and he will be mine, all mine. That is if I can finally convince him we are meant to be together and he should accept that fact.

I cannot wait! My dreams will soon become reality!

CHAPTER TWENTY-ONE

*W*hen Victoria woke, it was with a throbbing head and to a muffled, yet distinct, *whish-whoosh* soaring past her ears. Her eyes were blindfolded, her hands and feet were bound, and there was a coarse cloth shoved in her mouth. She tried to move, but couldn't. The space she was in was not only cramped, but vibrating. Over the whooshing, an engine revved.

Oh my God, Lord help me. I'm in a side cart of a motorcycle.

She had to fight off the sheer dark terror of being on the machine. Despite the terrible tenseness in her body and a misery hanging onto her like a steel weight, she slowly breathed in and out through her nose. If she let the panic coursing through her body consume her, she'd no doubt bawl and the gag would surely do its job and suffocate her. Following several breaths, an air of calm and self-confidence gradually returned.

A vehicle blared its horn close by them.

Oh God, don't let the car hit us. Don't let the cyclist crash. I so don't want to die like this. Her thoughts thrashed in a fretful maelstrom. The last traces of resistance and any progress she had made controlling her dread withered away. As her stomach knotted, she relived the final moments of her stalker boyfriend's death.

Dirt bikes and motorcycles had been Steve's passion. Posters of Harleys and races had covered the walls of his den. He'd once told her that from the age of eight, he had ridden almost every day in the fields and woods behind the family's home. When he turned thirteen, he entered competitions. He excelled, and after a few years, trophies filled every empty space in his parent's house. He had saved all his prize money he had received and with it bought a Harley Davidson instead of a car for his seventeenth birthday. It had come down with him to college. He had continued to compete while in school. His mother had always begged him to be careful while his father kept reminding their mother how experienced and competent a rider he was. He loved that bike.

Victoria had thought he was so cool when they first started dating. She hadn't minded riding with him either. There was an exhilaration to riding, a feeling of being free, reckless…dangerous. Who knew he'd carry it over into their relationship. As time wore on, he grew more possessive, belligerent, in their relationship. One night after he threatened to beat her if she didn't comply to his wishes, she told him in no uncertain terms she never wanted to see him again. That's when he started to stalk her.

Everywhere she went, there he was. He was always calling her, leaving notes on her car, passing messages through her friends to her. Some were loving, most weren't. A few times he showed up to her apartment and her neighbors called the cops on him due to screaming and banging on the door to be let in. It escalated to the point that she feared for her life. But without any true attempts made on her, there was nothing anyone could do.

Then one night, he caught up with her and some of her friends outside the Cowboy Café up in the hills. Foolish girl she was, she let him lure her away from her friends, then forced her to get on the bike and head off into the night with him by holding her at gunpoint. He sped them through the twists and turns of the hills. She knew the area, the road they were on. At one particular turn, he was forced to slow down and that's when she took a chance to escape by flinging herself off the bike.

She rolled away from him. Her clothes ripped and her skin shredded with road rash. Steve skidded to a stop several feet away, looking over his shoulder at her and revving the bike. She couldn't see his eyes due to the helmet and the dark, but she knew he wasn't pleased. Scrambling to her feet, she kept tabs on him. He spun the bike around. It stalled.

Fortunate for her. Bad for him.

Just as he restarted the motorcycle, a black Firebird came racing around the bend and slammed into him and his bike.

A scream had ripped from her throat. Steve's bike lay on the ground. He was under it. The car idled nearby.

When she regained her wits from the horror she witnessed, she limped her way over to the accident, then promptly wished she hadn't. Her stomach churned. Bile rose in her throat and burned her mouth.

Blood pooled around Steve's head, caking on his skin, helmet and leather. She froze to the spot and could only stare at Steve's lifeless form. Sirens from emergency response vehicles blared and stopped when they arrived.

Two medics picked up the motorcycle and moved it to the side.

Voices floated around her.

"We have a pulse on the female in the car," said one woman.

"Secure her and get her out," shouted a man in reply.

"You'll have to move away from here," said a cop.

She couldn't move for the life of her. She needed to see what happened to the man who'd made her life a living hell.

All the emergency personnel around him stood. One of the younger medics looked at his watch and pronounced the time of death.

Her friends, who'd called the police when they saw his gun and him force her away, showed up several moments later. They gave her support as she gave her report and followed the ambulance to the hospital where she got fixed up.

Ҽ҂Ҽ҂Ҽ҂

A few days later, she reviewed the accident report. The woman in the sports car had had a few drinks in her. She had been on the way to another bar after having dealt with hers and her soon to be ex-husband's divorce lawyers all day. When she had taken the curve, she was on the other side of the road where Steve had been.

Steve's whacky psychosis. The freaky motorcycle accident and the actions of the cops in regards to her complaints beforehand were why she hated both.

Panic rioted within her and she took another deep breath through her nose. She couldn't take being on the machine any longer, but there was nothing she could do to alter the situation. A spasmodic trembling took over her body, so she clenched each hand until her nails bit into her palms, hoping the pain in her fingers and skin would redirect her brain to stop the muscle contractions. Again, she slowly breathed through her nostrils. The stench of gasoline stung her nose.

Just as she made headway with composing herself, the vehicle slowed, then came to a stop. She took an extra careful breath of relief, struggling not to cry with joy that she had survived the ride.

Two hands groped around her, finding their way under her knees and in the middle of her back. Two arms followed and raised her from the seat. She was amazed the driver didn't have to peel her from the cart.

Carried for several steps, then thrown over her captor's shoulder, her midriff bounced against protuberances and the resulting exhalations from each impact seared her nasal cavities.

A door opened and a musty, dank stench overpowered the leather aroma of her kidnaper. Once placed on a chair, the helmet was removed from her head but not the blindfold.

"I'm sorry I haven't had time to clean this place," a male voice stated as he unbound her hands and feet. "If you're

good, I'll ungag you. Do you think you could be a good girl?"
He re-tied her hands and feet to the chair.

She nodded.

"Good. Good," he replied, tugging on the ropes. "If you're
so inclined to scream, you may and all you want. But it won't
do you any good. We're miles from the nearest town and the
closest cabin is a decent clip away and uninhabited at this
time."

The gritty cloth that had been shoved into her mouth was
pulled out. When she tried to speak, her tongue stuck to her
palate. Eventually she freed it and clucked it against her
parched membranes.

"Water?" Tori's hoarse voice cracked over the request.

"Ah, yes. You're probably thirsty. Let me get you a glass."

Footsteps clacked away. A pipe bellowed and hissed with
trapped air, then water ran. Footsteps tapped back.

"Here. I'm going to help you with this."

A cold glass was positioned on her bottom lip. She parted
her lips. He tipped the water into her mouth. The liquid was
stale and metallic. She sputtered and coughed. Cool wetness
trickled down the sides of her chin.

The footsteps clicked away, then back again. The captor
rubbed a cloth against her face. "You're a dirty one," he said
with a lewd chuckle. "If you really behave, I may even release
you from this chair and let you roam about when I step out
for errands. Granted, you'll be stuck within these walls. The
door is locked from the outside, and only I have the key. All
the windows are boarded so there's no chance of escape."

* * * *

"We should have gone to the police sooner. But we didn't.
Now she's gone, and for all we know, she's dead."

Geoff, caught off guard by Sally's distraught declarations,
merely stared at the woman, amazed and very shaken,
momentarily speechless in his surprise.

"I've called the police and told them to meet us here in your office. They already know my side of the story since I was there yesterday. I'm hoping you might be able to help them as well. Give them some clue as to where she could be or who would do anything to her."

"Sally, have a seat," he said, indicating a chair in front of his desk. "I'm so sorry to hear about your dog. And, I know about the notes. Tori showed them to me the night of the banquet. But as for who is behind all that, I have no idea."

"Not even an inkling?" she asked in a choked voice.

"Nope. None. And, please, don't think for a moment that Tori's dead. She's strong and smart. She's a survivor."

"Um, Geoff?" Philip poked his head into the office. "There's a couple of cops here looking for you."

Geoff looked to Sally who inclined her head.

"Send them in," he replied. As Philip opened the door and showed the men in, Geoff rose from his desk to greet the officers. "Good day. I'm Geoff McKenzie and this is Sally Becker, the one who called you here."

"I'm Officer Abrams and this is my partner Officer Kent," the taller of the two uniformed men offered. "I'm sure you know we're here to ask you some questions in regards to the disappearance of Victoria Padden."

"Yes, I'm aware of that," Geoff replied. "Phil, could you get some chairs from the front for the gentlemen?"

"When was the last time you saw Ms. Padden, Mr. McKenzie?" Officer Kent asked once the chairs had been brought in and they had taken their seats.

Philip quietly left the room and shut the door behind him.

"Two nights ago," Geoff replied. "She and I went to a banquet, then back to her house."

"Can anyone confirm this?" Officer Abrams submitted.

"Sure. Anyone who was at the event can," he answered back in a facile tongue.

"What about at her house?"

"My friend and limo driver, Pete Wolowsky."

Both officers took a moment to jot down the information in their miniature notebooks.

"Does Ms. Padden have any enemies?" Officer Kent continued with the questioning. "Anyone she is in dispute with?"

"Enemies?" Geoff glanced at Sally who shrugged her shoulders then looked back at the policemen. "I don't believe she had any. She never mentioned anyone hating her that much."

"There is Linda," Sally interjected.

"Who's Linda?" The officers, in unison, directed their question to the woman.

"Linda Moore. She's an employee of mine and a co-worker of Tori's. Linda's a bit of the jealous type and has been feeling slighted because of Tori's advancements at work. Linda doesn't hide the fact that she's annoyed with her either."

"You're right. Tori had a bit of a run in with her that night. She had a…umm… *discussion* with Gertrude Sims too."

"Do you know what these discussions were about?" asked the tall officer.

"Unfortunately, no. All I know is that they upset her enough that she ran out of the hall. I had to chase her down. I ended up taking her home."

"How about you, Mr. McKenzie?" inquired Officer Kent.

"How about me what?"

The officers looked at each other. Officer Abrams nodded his head and then Officer Kent produced a file from his briefcase. He pulled some papers from the folder and laid them on the desk in front of Geoff.

"These are copies of notes we found in Ms. Padden's bag which was located on her property." Officer Kent said, leaning forward and lowering his voice. "We assume she didn't just disappear, but was abducted and had dropped the bag when she was taken."

ক্ষ্জ্বক্ষ্জ্বক্ষ্জ্ব

Sally gasped and slapped a hand over her heart.

"From the looks of these notes," Officer Kent continued. "It seems someone didn't want the two of you together. So, Mr. McKenzie, I'm asking, do you have any enemies or those who may have a grudge against you?"

Geoff sat back in his chair and studied the officers. Victoria kidnapped? He tried not to be relieved over the fact that she had been snatched away, but he couldn't help it. She hadn't run off like all the other women in his life had. This time there had been a reason for a girlfriend's disappearance. Then again, maybe what was happening now could explain those other times as well. "As far as I know I have no enemies. I can name a handful of people, though, who might not be happy I'm dating her."

"Please, give us all the names you can think of no matter how trivial you think the connection may be."

"Like Sally said, there's Linda. Then there's Tori's ex-boyfriend David Lloyd. She recently moved out of his house and planned to turn down his marriage proposal. Then there's Bertha Sims. Her mother, Gertrude, has tried relentlessly to set me up with Bertha and Bertha has been involved with her mother's schemes as well. Then there's my son."

"Your son?" Sally asked incredulously. "Since when do you have a son?"

Three pairs of eyes stared at him, silently questioning.

"Since yesterday," he responded. "My ex-wife stopped by late in the morning and dropped the life changing news on my lap. She'd deserted our marriage years ago, and it was because she was pregnant. I never knew. Well, it turns out he went missing from the school he boards at. She thought he finally tried to contact me. She says he's bitter, feels I had something to do with her leaving me when she's repeatedly told him that's not the case."

"What are your ex-wife's and son's names and do you have contact numbers for them?" Abrams asked.

"Sue Ellen Mills and Zachary Mills. And, yes, I have numbers for Sue Ellen." Geoff picked up the business card she had given him from beside the phone and handed it to Officer Kent.

"Good. Thank you." He stood and Officer Abrams followed suit. "Thank you both for your time. We'll be sure to look into the names you provided us and when we learn of anything we'll let you know."

Geoff saw the officers out, and when he returned to his desk, he sat with a weary sigh.

"So now what do we do?" Sally asked wringing her hands together.

"Nothing, I guess, but wait," he answered, his words filled with uneasy worry.

A throat cleared.

Geoff looked up and Sally turned to see Officer Abrams standing in the doorway.

"We just got a call," the officer stated tersely. "We need you both to come down to the station."

CHAPTER TWENTY-TWO

A cell phone trilled several feet from Victoria. Her kidnapper shoved a gritty cloth into her mouth, then stepped away.

"Hello?" he answered. "Who is this? How did you get my number? Oh, really now? Is that so?" There was a long pause. "Interesting. Very interesting. I'll take care of things. Don't worry."

Footsteps approached her.

"My, aren't you a pretty sight all trussed up," he said as he cupped a breast.

Tori cringed. She had no idea who the man was. He had yet to unbind her eyes and release the ties around her wrists and ankles. She had no perception of how long she had been held captive. The man was no help, not bothering to answer any of her questions. All he told her was when to eat, sleep, and go to the bathroom. He would untie her and then rebind her so she'd be able to walk and move but not escape. And having to use the facilities was the most humiliating part of the whole experience. She could swear he watched her do her business, considering he groaned each time she pulled down her jeans and panties and sat on the toilet.

She didn't know how much longer she could endure being stuck here, especially when his touches were becoming more sexual.

"I have to step out for a little while," he continued. "But when I return, we'll have some special time together and I'll free you in more ways than one."

His footsteps clacked away. The door squeaked open, then slammed shut. The sound of metal against metal clicked.

* * * *

Geoff and Sally followed Officers Abrams and Kent down a long corridor and into a small sterile room with only a table and a few chairs as furnishings. There were two plain clothed detectives watching a young woman through a window in the wall. The woman appeared distraught.

"That's her," Geoff exclaimed when he got a good look at her. "That's the girl from the restaurant."

"What restaurant?" one of the detectives turned to ask.

"The other night when Victoria and I went out to eat that girl kept staring at us. It really unnerved Tori."

"Was she with anyone?" The detective jerked a thumb at the window.

"Yeah, but we never saw who her female companion was."

The man turned to his partner. They looked at each other, then left the room. A couple of minutes later, they emerged on the other side of the window with each taking a place alongside the table and girl.

Officer Abrams flipped a switch on the wall stating it would allow them to hear what the men and woman said.

"Tell Officer White and I again about Ms. Padden and Mr. McKenzie," the cop on the right requested.

"Look, I told you guys. I never met the woman or Zach's dad."

At the mention of his son's name, Geoff hissed through his teeth. Sally placed a hand on his arm.

"All I know is," the girl continued, "that when I heard my uncle on the phone with Zach's friend, I got worried that our harmless pranks weren't so harmless anymore. I had no clue that my uncle knew what was going on or that it would go this far. As for Zach, I don't know where he is. When I told him I was going to call the police, he took off on his dirt bike. And if I had known you were going treat me like I've done something wrong, I never would have come in."

"Well, Detective Sullivan and I just heard news," the officer on the left commented. "Tell us about the restaurant you went to the other night and the woman you were with. Why you were staring at Ms. Padden and Mr. McKenzie?"

"My uncle never told me that was them," the girl muttered.

"Uncle? I thought you were with a woman?" White reacted, placing his hands upon the table and leaning toward her.

The girl didn't reply. She kept her head down and played with her nails.

"We understand," Detective Sullivan said, pulling out a chair from the table and swinging it around to sit on it so its back was against his chest. "Your fear and reluctance to expose your friends and family, but if you know something more, anything at all, we need to know it, too. A woman has been taken against her will and may be in danger. We need you to help us help her."

"This is embarrassing," she muttered, still keeping her head lowered. "My uncle is a woman now. Or at least is on his way to becoming one. He's been dressing like a woman and getting shots at the doctor's office for a few years. He's waiting on a letter of approval so he can be scheduled for surgery in a couple of months. He's a brilliant man, but when it comes to love I guess you can say he has a screw loose or two. A handful of years ago he started seeing this therapist and fell hard for the guy. It was really weird seeing my uncle crush over some dude. But to each his own." She shrugged a shoulder.

"When the therapist turned down his advances, he was upset. But then the counselor guy had to go and say that, if my uncle had been a female, things may have been different. With that bit of hope my uncle stopped seeing the guy and began his transformation process expecting to hook up with him again when it's complete. Recently he found out the guy is engaged. That tweaked him really bad. So with him not being quite right at times, I tend to do what he asks. No need to make him worse than he already is, ya know? And people think only women are hormonal. Try living with a man getting shots of the stuff."

"So what does this have to do with the couple in question?" White asked.

"How the hell should I know?" she asked, jerking her head up and glaring at the man. "All I know is when we got to the restaurant, he started to pitch a fit about a couple who were out on a date. He told me to keep an eye on them and tell him what they were doing. I didn't bother to ask for details. When he gets into states like that, questions only tend to make the matter worse. I chalked it up to his hormone therapy and watched the couple for him."

"Could you tell us the names your uncle goes by and if you happen to remember the therapist's name?" Sullivan questioned.

"My uncle used to be named Lynden Coors. He now goes by Linda Moore. And the therapist was Lloyd something or other."

In the other room, Sally collapsed into a chair and fanned herself with a hand.

"Do you think she's talking about David?" Geoff asked in a strained voice, concerned how pale Sally had become and fearing for Tori's safety and life.

"Yes, the girl's talking about David. And Linda is Tori's co-worker. This can't be good."

* * * *

Several hours later, Tori woke to the soft sound of rhythm and blues playing in the background and the aroma of Chinese take-out. The familiar gait of her kidnapper's footfall thumped on the floor, coming close to her.

"So beautiful," he whispered in her ear, his breath hot and moist, against her skin. He unbuttoned her top and pushed the fabric to the sides, exposing her chest and beige push-up bra. "Very beautiful."

She shuddered. If the gag wasn't in her mouth, she'd take him up on his earlier offer and scream.

"Oh, darlin', there's no reason to be nervous with me," he crooned and placed a kiss along the baseline of her jaw. "I don't plan to hurt you…much. But it'll be only a little pain, and after it's over, all you'll feel is pleasure." He traced a finger along the top of her right breast, then along her bra. "Now, if you'll agree to be a good girl, I'll take the gag out and feed you some of the food I picked up. Will you be good for me?"

She nodded her head vehemently.

"I thought so," he replied pulling the coarse cloth out of her mouth.

"Thank you," she croaked after taking a refreshing breath of air. Her throat was dry, and not wanting to lose her voice, she decided not to scream. Instead she asked, "Why did you undo my shirt?"

"You're a bit messy when you eat and I didn't think you wanted to ruin your blouse any more than it already has been," he stated. "Besides, I wanted a view with my dinner." He cupped her left breast and gave it a squeeze.

She squirmed and he released her. The clack of his footsteps retreated and came back. A paper bag rustled.

"So would you like to start with the Lo Mein or the Lemon Chicken? I think we'll start with the Lemon Chicken. It'd be much easier to feed you pieces of meat," he chuckled, "than the messy noodles."

A knife scrapped several times on what she assumed was the container for the food. Her mouth watered. As much as she hated him feeding her, she was hungry. He hadn't fed or given her water in hours which she figured was a blessing. The less she ate or drank, the less she'd have to use the facilities and have him benefit from an unsolicited peep show.

After feeding her a few pieces, he heaved a heavy sigh.

"What?" she asked with a bit of concern, fearing if something were to happen to him she may never get back home.

"You've seemed to have gotten a bit of sauce on yourself."

"I don't feel anything."

Right as those words finished leaving her mouth, he trailed a path with his tongue into the cleft of her breasts. As he traced a path over the top of the left one, he removed the right one from the bra cup and fondled it with a heavy hand.

Apprehension welled up inside her, but it would do no good if she were to lose her cool. In the back of her mind, she had the idea that she had to remain calm and not fight the situation because fighting could aggravate her aggressor and put her in a worse predicament. She couldn't help the repulsion that coursed through her veins when his lips found purchase on her nipple. She trembled and tried to pull away from him.

"Oh, there's no need to be shy with me," he said after he stopped sucking. He placed a hand on her thigh and rubbed it up the length of her leg to the juncture between. He gave her crotch a squeeze through her jeans. "You know you want this. You know you want me," he pushed his whole hand up against her groin and kneaded the area as his mouth fastened onto her breast again.

Keep calm, she told herself. If an opportunity from this presents itself you may have a chance to escape.

"Mmmm, so tasty." He popped her other breast out of its confines and gave its tip a lick. "But I think your first time shouldn't be on a chair, don't you? We'll move this little party over to the bed. What do you think?"

Move? Could this be the chance she had wished for? She had to play her cards right with this.

"Sure. The bed sounds wonderful," she agreed in the sultriest voice she could conjure considering she felt nowhere near sexy with this character.

He gave a gleeful, yet vulgar, giggle and began to undo her binds.

She waited patiently, hoping in his aroused state he would forget to tighten the ropes when she was free from the chair. As the moments passed, it occurred to her what he had last said. First time. Did the man somehow have it in his head she was a virgin?

At last the binds were loose and the areas where the cords had bound her tingled with the rush of fresh blood. When he stood her on her feet, she fell forward into his arms, and she realized the binds on her wrists and ankles were very loose. Loose enough to free herself.

"Ah, darlin', you're right where I want you. In my arms and close to me," his voice rumbled lecherously.

"That's nice," she replied, gently shucking the ropes from her hands behind her. "But I'm afraid I have some bad news."

"Bad news?" he asked, still gripping the upper parts of her arms tightly.

"Yeah, whoever gave you the idea I'm a virgin was sadly mistaken. I'm nowhere near a virgin and you would be far from my first man."

Her captor pushed her away, growled in frustration, then backhanded her across the face.

She fell onto the chair, her hands freed, and as she made it back on her feet, she held on to the piece of furniture. The blindfold had moved just enough from the force of the slap that she could see the man's feet. When he began to rush toward her, she hauled the chair up into the air and slammed it down in his direction.

There was a loud *thunk* and chunks of wood tumbling on the floor.

She lifted the cover off her eyes and stared at the unmoving mass of man on the ground. With the stick remains of the chair in her hand, she poked at him and flipped him over. Her panting breaths stopped.

࿐ ࿐ ࿐ ࿐ ࿐ ࿐

Buck lay there motionless.

She had no time to sit and ponder the situation and figure out why Sally's landscaper had abducted her and brought her to the cabin she was in. She had to get out and fast, before he woke and really hurt her.

Bending down, she pawed his pockets and found a set of keys. She grabbed them from his unresponsive body and ran to the door. Her fingers shook and it took several attempts to find the right key, get it in the lock and get the door open. Once outside, she slammed the door and relocked it.

Her chest heaved with the exertion and fright of the experience. As she scanned the area, she righted her bra and breasts, and buttoned her shirt. In the distance, a stream of smoke rose from within the trees.

She weaved and stumbled down the road toward it.

CHAPTER TWENTY-THREE

"**V**ictoria, sweetie, that's it. Open your eyes," a gentle voice crooned in the darkness.

And, though she tried to fight waking, her eyelids fluttered opened. As Tori roused, she became aware of a tight throbbing in her left arm, an incessant beeping near the same side's ear. Geoff and Sally stared down at her.

"Where am I?" Her voice was rough and crackly, her throat dry and scratchy. "Where's Buck? What's going on?"

The bleeps picked up speed.

"Shh, calm down," Geoff soothed as he sat beside her. "You're in Hunterdon Med. You're all right now. Buck is in jail."

"You gave us quite a scare, young lady," Sally said and took a place on the other side of the bed. "You were unconscious for two nights and we thought you were heading for a third."

"Really? I'm sorry," she said apologetic, feeling bad for causing them any worry. She glanced around the private mint green hospital room. The glaring white lights above her hummed.

"There's nothing to apologize for. The doctors said you were dehydrated, exhausted and suffering from a bit of post-traumatic stress. It was only natural for you to have shut down for a period of time."

"Oh, okay." She shifted her position in the bed and winced at the pain from her wrists and ankles. "So Buck's in jail? Do you know why he went after me in the first place?"

Geoff and Sally exchanged a look.

"Come on guys, I have a right to know," Tori asserted thinking since she was the one who went through the trauma she should at least understand the reasoning behind it.

"Well, it seems that my son, Zach, didn't like growing up without me," Geoff began.

"Excuse me?" Tori exclaimed, astonished at this blow of news. "Your son?"

"Yeah, it came as a shock to me, too. Sue Ellen showed up on my front porch a few days ago and informed me he was missing. He was the reason she left me all those years ago. She was afraid I wouldn't be available to help her raise him so she took off. Turns out he was more bitter than she had thought. Zach craved my attention, wanted me all for himself. He was the one who tormented my girlfriends with the same kind of notes and threats you had received. Seems that my boy is a bit of a genius when it comes to computers. He knows how to hack his way in to almost any system and find out anything he wants or needs to know on anything or anyone. Zach traced my ex-girlfriends. That's why they all left me. He tracked you, too, knew your past and how to get to you."

Tori's whole body shook. She couldn't believe people would go to such lengths. The situation had been dire, and she was lucky she made it out of there. The machine next to her increased the time between beeps. She shook her head and breathed deep, attempting to calm herself before her vitals became a concern. "Is Sue Ellen tall and blonde?"

"Yeah, she is," he answered. "How'd you know?"

"I was across the street when she showed up that day," she stated as she shifted in the bed, then winced at the pain at the bottom of her legs.

"Why didn't you come to the house?"

"After I saw Gertrude and Bertha leave then some model-type arrive, I decided against bothering you. You seemed really happy to see her. I was supposed to meet Sally at the station within a set timeframe, and I was running late. Buck must have been in on the scheme, too. He almost raped me."

"He did what?" Geoff bellowed.

"He didn't get far," Tori assured him, placing her right hand against his cheek. "At that point I was free and was able to subdue him."

"Good," Geoff snarled. "Otherwise, I would have had to take a trip to the station."

"The cops will have to be informed of what he attempted to do to her," Sally reminded them. "But as for Buck, turns out he got around quite a bit. He worked at the school Zach goes to and that's how they became friends. He figured he'd help Zach with his plans because he was happy they were buddies. Buck wanted to be accepted and cared about by somebody…anybody."

"Speaking of the other day, what was the deal with the Simses?" Tori shifted, annoyed at all the wires and machines monitoring her every blip and gurgle.

"I told them I was serious about you and to make up for Gertrude's trouble I offered to put a free fountain in her garden," Geoff remarked. "That appeased her. As for Bertha, turns out she'd met someone else and had been keeping the relationship from her mother so as not to upset her."

"That would explain the sappy look I saw on her face."

"That it would. Zach also had another friend who would help him deliver the notes," Geoff continued. "Allie was the one who finally contacted the police about their schemes when she overheard Linda on the phone with Buck telling him he should compromise you. Because then David wouldn't want you anymore if you were used goods."

"Used goods? Wow, I guess acting like a prude really came in handy. When I told Buck he wouldn't be my first, he threw a fit. But, why should Linda care about David or my sex life? And how'd she get hooked up with Buck and Zach?"

Geoff's cell phone rang. He looked at the screen. "I need to take this call. Sally, you can have the honors of telling her this part." He rose from the bed and stepped out into the hall.

"Because Linda has a thing for David or I should say *Lynden* has the hots for David."

"Sally, you're not making any sense," Tori grimaced and again tried to find a comfortable position on the thin mattress hospital bed.

"Linda is actually a man named Lynden. Lynden saw David in a professional manner when David was interning and fell for him. Since David normally isn't attracted to males, he turned Lynden down but said, if he had been a lady, then a relationship could have been possible. Lynden took that to heart and took steps to make the transformation. He changed his look, changed his career, and fooled me into thinking he was a lady. I know her voice has always been deep for a gal, but I just figured she had been a smoker once upon a time. His…umm… her seeing David and falling for him is why she…umm…he disliked you so much when you got the account where David has his office and started dating him. Then when word of the proposal got out, Lynden lost it. He felt he was so close to his prize and then to have it ripped away caused him to break down mentally. So when he got wind of what his niece was up to, he joined in the fiasco. He figured he'd help out Buck and Zach. By tormenting you, you'd leave Geoff, and if enough happened, David wouldn't want you anymore either. Both men would then be available. Lynden's being held at the station along with Zach, whom the authorities were finally able to catch. And here we are."

"Oh my God, Sally." Tori rubbed her temples and wondered how she was ever going to process all this strange information. "Does David know about Linda? I mean Lynden. Does he know about me? I still have to talk to him. Is there a phone I can use? What about your dog?"

శ్రార్ధిర్యార్ధిర్యా

"Relax, Tori," her friend crooned. "Snowpea is fine. He was with Allie and was well taken care of. David is fully aware of what happened. He sends his regards and hopes you don't mind that he wants to rescind his proposal. He confessed to me he was pushing for a commitment with you so he wouldn't have to face what he truly wanted deep down, which was a relationship with Lynden. He says that's why he's been so weird. He had been fighting with the truth of his feelings and losing the battle." Sally shrugged.

Tori gave a short chuckle. "Are there any other secrets lurking out there that I need to be aware of?"

"Only one," Geoff said, returning to the side of her bed with the phone still against his ear.

"Great. Let's have it." She sank into the pillows behind her back and head, closed her eyes and resigned herself to possibility of more bad news. She took a deep breath, then gazed at Geoff. "I don't think I can be any more surprised than I have been already."

"The last secret I have to share," he said with a smile, "is that I love you, and if your parents give me permission, I'd like to ask you to marry me."

Over the phone a woman shrieked and a man cheered.

"Are those my parents?" The machine attached to Tori bleeped.

"Yep. They wanted to check in and see how you were doing. What?" He directed the question into the phone. "Is that a yes? I have your permission?"

Geoff smiled at Victoria and nodded.

"Then," she said, "I need to tell you my final secret as well."

He covered the mouthpiece of the phone. "Yes?"

"I love you, too. So my answer is yes."

Another shout came through the phone and Sally clapped in approval.

"Geoff, I'll marry you under one condition."

He quirked an eyebrow. "Name it."

"No more secrets."

EPILOGUE

"**G**eoff you really shouldn't be in this room right now." Victoria dashed behind a four paneled Venetian room divider screen set up so she would have a private area to change in when others were present. "Don't you know it's bad luck to see the bride before the wedding? What if Sally or my mother catch you in here?" She peeked around the side at Geoff who was still dressed in a pair of jeans and a flannel shirt looking like he had just come off a job.

He grinned and locked the door. "Is that better? As for that superstition, let's pretend it doesn't exist. Now come out from behind there. I want to kiss my bride to be."

Tori giggled. "Okay, only one small kiss. No funny business. I have to look stunning for my wedding which is only a couple of hours away." She skipped out from behind the partition.

"What's this? Sweats and a sweat shirt? You're not even in the dress so what were you worried about?" He took her in his arms and kissed her forehead.

"You're not supposed to see me." She rubbed her cheek against his chest.

"It's unlucky for the groom to see the bride in her whole wedding dress before the ceremony. That doesn't mean I can't see you. And since you're nowhere near dressed in your wedding outfit, we're okay."

"And how do you know about such a girly thing?"

"Aunt Cheryl. You're sure only a little kiss?"

"Well, we are in an ancillary room of the church. We have our families milling about trying to get ready for the service.

We need to get ready for—"

He swooped his mouth down on hers, brushing his lips against hers with broad strokes.

"I love you, Victoria. I'll love you till the day I die."

"I know," she whispered back and kissed his chin. "I feel the same way."

He placed his lips upon hers again, lightly feathering his touch upon her mouth. After several moments the gentle, sweet kiss turned into a demanding, passionate melding. He clutched her back, pinning her tight against him. A shiver ran through him when he realized this kiss was much more intense and heartfelt than the other ones he had shared with her. The change was probably because he did truly love her and in a few hours she would be his for eternity. He knew deep down his marriage to Tori would last. A low growl hummed in his throat as he fought to rid his mind of all thought and concentrate on the woman in his arms. His teeth nicked her lips, his tongue caressed hers. Warmth blanketed his body and enveloped his spirit. A wave of hungry desire spiraled through him. His lips continued to claim hers in a savage intensity.

In each other's arms, they knelt on the floor as their mouths and tongues warred. He laid her back upon the floor, spread his length over her, and not allowing her any kind of escape, continued to kiss her. He couldn't get enough of her and his searing need overrode the fact that they were in a church and that at any moment people could find a key and barge in on them. Everyone could hang for all he cared. All he wanted was the woman under him, the woman who held him in his arms. He threw his all into the kiss as if to devour her and felt her matching passionate response to him. For several long moments, he enjoyed her, then ended the kiss and rested his forehead upon hers.

"God, Tori, I want you so much."

"I kind of gathered that," she replied breathlessly.

He returned his mouth to hers, more demanding this time, as he straddled her and cupped her cheeks. Her response seemed eager and she shuddered beneath his fingers. Oh, how he wanted to claim more from her than just her mouth. He wanted to explore every inch of her. Trailing his kisses from her mouth to one side of her chin and then the other, he guided his hand around to the front of her body and to her breast.

"Oh, Geoff."

Geoff never believed his name could hold so much emotion and let out a long, audible breath, pulling his body from hers. Like the first time he had made love to her, his words failed him. He wanted her so much, and since he seemed unable to express himself verbally when caught in his passion, he let his eyes and facial expression convey his feelings.

When she gazed at him with her beautiful blue eyes, his breath caught in his throat. "Tell me again, Victoria. Tell me you love me."

"I love you, Geoff. Very much."

Above them in the church tower the bells rang.

"As much as I'd love to be here with you, Geoff, you really should get going before my mother, Sally and the rest of the ladies return from their manicures."

"Mmm, maybe you're right." He wrapped her in his arms, kissed her again.

Tori molded into him, then thinking better of the situation, pushed him from her.

"Okay, okay. I get the hint."

A loud knock sounded at the door. Tori stared at Geoff, puckered her lips, raised her eyebrows, and put her hand and arm out toward the door in a silent way of saying *See, I told you so.*

"Tori, why is this door locked?" Sally inquired from the other side.

Once she sat at the table where her mirror and hairbrush were, Geoff opened the door.

"Good afternoon, ladies."

Felicia and Sally rushed inside straight to Tori's side.

Aunt Cheryl snickered. "So this is why you asked me about the wedding superstitions. Come on. My son's been looking for you."

"What was he doing in here?" Felicia Padden asked as she took the brush from Victoria and began brushing her hair.

"Your nails, Mom."

"They're dry. Now answer my question."

"Yes, Tori, what was he doing in here?" Sally joined in with a wink.

"He came to see me. It's all right. It's only bad if he sees me in my dress before I walked down the aisle."

"Gosh, Victoria, you have your whole life ahead of you to see him all you want. You two couldn't wait a couple of hours?"

Victoria looked at her mother via the woman's reflection in the mirror and shrugged a shoulder.

"And look at you," Felicia continued. "You're not even part way ready. We'd thought you'd at least have your makeup and hair done by now. I really wish you would have had a longer engagement, planned to have your wedding back home. We could have had hair and makeup artists come in for you. There's that beautiful cathedral. Then the banquet hall at—"

"Stop, Mother." Tori put down her makeup brush. "This area is my home now and we didn't want a big, flashy wedding. Plain and simple is how we're going and I would hope you'd be happy for me."

"I am happy for you. I just had my own visions of this day I guess."

"I know you did, Mom, but this is my day, isn't it?"

Felicia nodded as she finished putting Victoria's hair up in a French twist and added sprigs of Baby's Breath to the hairstyle. Tori finished the last touches of her makeup.

"Here's your dress, Tori." Sally held up the beautiful gown.

The beaded lace mermaid gown with bolero jacket and chapel train was the one item for her wedding she didn't cheap out on. The dress, fitted at the top and flaring below the knee, conformed to her body perfectly and the cropped jacket added a nice touch. The train extended only about four feet from the waist, but she loved it since she'd have no fear of tripping on it.

Tori took the outfit from Sally, went behind the screen, and moments later, stepped out with it on. Both Felicia and Sally had tears in their eyes. Both exclaimed how beautiful she was. Her mother hugged her and then fastened the back of the gown.

Another knock sounded at the door and Tori hurried behind the screen to be on the safe side.

Her father's voice rumbled from the doorway. Tori stepped out. In the distance *Canon in D* played on the organ.

"It's time, Victoria," Robert Padden offered his daughter his arm. The group of them left the room.

Her mother led the way and was seated by an usher. Sally strolled down the aisle resplendent in a dark red sleeveless gown and went to stand across from Geoff and Philip on the other side of the minister.

Victoria smiled brightly as her gaze stayed fixed on the man of her dreams. She hoped he wouldn't be too disappointed that Sally didn't get them a gift. After all, she did tell her friend that despite all the trouble attached to it, she had already given them a gift, the chance to meet at a bachelor auction and fall in love.

ABOUT THE AUTHOR

Casey Moss delves into the darker aspects of life in her writing, sometimes basing the stories on reality, sometimes on myth. No matter the path, her stories will take you on a journey from the light-hearted paranormal to dark things unspeakable. *What waits around the corner?* Come explore…

For more about the author and her stories, visit
http://caseymossbooks.com/

www.ingramcontent.com/pod-product-compliance
Lightning Source LLC
Chambersburg PA
CBHW060916180626
46817CB00004B/1275